VANISHED IN VISTA POINT

A FORENSICS 411 MYSTERY

WHITNEY SKEEN

FAWKES PRESS

Copyright © 2020 Whitney V. Skeen

All rights reserved.

No part of this book may be reproduced in any form or by any electronic or
mechanical means, including information storage and retrieval systems, without
written permission from the author, except for the use of brief quotations in a
book review.

Edited by Twyla Beth Lambert

Cover design by Fresh Design

Cover illustrations by Moran Reudor

Print ISBN 978-1-945419-59-1

Ebook ISNB 978-1-945419-70-6

LCCN 2020930174

This book is a work of fiction. Names, characters, businesses, places, events,
locales, and incidents are either the products of the author's imagination or used
in a fictitious manner. Any resemblance to actual persons, living or dead, or
actual events is purely coincidental. Brand names are the property of the
respective companies; author and publisher hold no claim.

ACKNOWLEDGMENTS

Thank you to my husband, Todd, for his unending support and encouragement as I pursued the dream of writing this book.

To my beta readers Coralie Hegben-Brink, Emily Cupp, Sara Cupp, Lien Lancaster, Rebecca Lee, Mary Tobin, Kim Turbyfill, Lane Turbyfill, Meredith Verdin, and Mrs. Angie Fleming's sixth graders at North Rowan Middle School: I am incredibly grateful for your interest, support and help in bringing this story to life.

To my agent Patty Carothers and my editors Twylabeth Lambert and Jodi Thompson, thank you for investing in what I created in Hank, Hannah, and Chaucer.

Finally, to my readers, thank you for picking this book to be part of your life. You have not heard the last from the kids of Vista Point.

While many of Hank's webisodes
are based on real cases and solid forensic evidence,
others take creative liberty
for the sake of the story.

In other words, readers who use this book
as a manual to solve (or commit) crimes
may find themselves disappointed
by the outcome.

1

F *orensics is the use of science to investigate criminal activity and analyze evidence as it relates to the law. In short, a forensic investigation can help determine if a person died as a result of criminal harm, while also applying scientific methods to help identify possible perpetrators of the crime.* See Forensics 411 *episode 1, "The Basics."*

THE BUS.

Talk about crime scenes!

I hated the bus.

The noises, the smells, the over-crowded conditions—it had all the disadvantages of a school hallway without the benefit of climate control.

The only tolerable thing about the bus was that fifty percent of the time it took me *away* from school. The best place to be in relation to Vista Point Middle School was away. Learning, I loved, but school was a daily dose of mandatory anguish.

I put in my earbuds, mostly for protection, then cued my bus playlist. Swaddled in my music cocoon, I scrolled through messages on my *Forensics 411* social media feeds. My subscribers were faithful, if not large in number. They loved my riveting forensic videos, crime blog, and quick response time. If my new interactive features went well, I'd have a thousand followers by the end of summer and be one step closer to getting a corporate sponsor. Investigation Innovations or Corpse Corps were my dream sponsors, but I'd settle for a second-rate fabric softener. You've got to start somewhere.

I scrolled through comments from familiar names to a message from someone named `GirlofSteel`. A new follower? I smiled and read her message: `I think someone was murdered in my house. Can u help?`

My heart sped up. A real murder to investigate? I stared out the bus window and pictured myself, Henry "Boomer" Boyd, more widely known as the detective from *Forensics 411*, at a crime scene in full protective gear, bent over a dead body, combing the site for trace evidence. A photographer behind me snapping pictures of the body while a minion put up yellow crime scene tape.

I glanced around at the other inmates locked behind the yellow doors of doom. Dillon Buckley (screen name `TheBuckster`) perched in his assigned seat in the first row facing backward. It was a clear violation of system-wide transportation rules, but the bus driver ignored him. I wished I could.

Dillon flashed an insufferable smirk in my direction.

I typed: `Really?` to `GirlofSteel` and watched Dillon. A second later he pulled his phone from his pocket and swiped the screen.

I growled to myself then answered "GirlofSteel." `If this is a true medical emergency, please hang up and dial 911,` then hit "send."

Of course, a real murder was too good to be true. I never caught a break like that.

Dillon Buckley loved to mess with me. It was like a sport for him. Knowing Dillon's older brother and cousin, I'd long suspected a genetic predisposition to bullying in the Buckley family. Crazy as it sounds, it's a thing. I plan to make a *Forensics 411* episode about it someday—when the subject doesn't hit so close to home.

Dillon was everything an adversary should be. His accomplished dishonesty, intellectual inferiority, and infuriating athleticism were equally offensive. Throw in his ability to deliver an impeccable atomic wedgie and his obnoxious arrogance, and the jack-wagon was absolutely revolting. Probably tortured puppies!

Over the years, my therapist, Dr. Blanchard, has said to ignore Dillon. For a hundred and sixty bucks an hour, I think Dr. B could come up with something more innovative than that. My mom (and the school counselor) gave me the same advice, no charge.

FYI—it didn't work.

Like a mosquito bite on your finger, you couldn't ignore Dillon. He wouldn't allow it.

And by the curse of the alphabet, I couldn't escape him. He was never more than two seats away.

Since my extreme reaction to a fire drill in kindergarten, I've been his target. An ill-timed boomerang toss in first grade turned his occasional harassments into regular attacks planned with precision and malice.

Once Dillon took aim at me, chronic unpopularity set in. The other kids went along with him; the alternative was that he'd turn on *them*. It's classic social Darwinism. The human instinct to survive trumps kindness, empathy or even decency.

For Dillon, I was low-hanging fruit—the limping caribou at the back of the pack.

Dr. Blanchard said I was the "smart brown kid" that Dillon, for some reason, considered a threat. I liked his spin much better than being a lame caribou or a sagging apple.

In sixth grade, it became necessary for me to do independent study at home. Without a teacher having to spend so much time telling kids like Dillon to shut up and behave, learning went remarkably fast. In my spare time, I found solace in crime.

I didn't commit it, I studied it—and its victims.

I was the only kid who knew the signs of thallium poisoning, the intricacies of ballistics testing, and the shortcomings of luminol. After several months of round-the-clock reading and research, I went public with a forensic web show and blog known as *Forensics 411*. In no time, I was the twenty-third most popular crime and forensic blogger on the web.

The bus ground to a stop. As I forced my way through the shoulders and backpacks, I passed `TheBuckster`. He let one rip, waved his hand in front of his face and said, "Nasty Forensic Freak! Time to change your not-so-tidy-whities!" *Well-played Buckley! You conjure a fart, then question my mother's laundering skills. Brilliant. I totally get why you're so popular!*

My bus driver muttered, "Have a good one," and shut the doors, spewing a cloud of diesel fumes in my face as she drove away.

I reached in my pocket and squeezed the remnants of the stress ball Dr. Blanchard prescribed for Dillon dealings or other emotionally taxing times. Squishing the foam was supposed to be a sensory reminder not to engage with him. I liked to picture the foam as his head smashed between my two omnipotent fingertips.

I inhaled the salt breeze blowing off the waterway and let it wash over me for three sacred seconds of peace. Then, I headed home.

The school year was over. I survived eighth grade and had a 77-day hiatus from the government-sanctioned, tax-payer-supported dystopia known as middle school. High school lurked at the end of summer as a fortress to conquer, or a stomach virus to endure. My greatest hope for high school was to become the guy in the corner that nobody noticed. Online, I would build on my success.

Until late August there would be no bus, no school, and none of what came with it. I'd enjoy life, perfect some new boomerang tricks, and ramp up production of new *Forensics 411* episodes. My fans were waiting.

While I walked up the street, I scrolled through more messages. "Yes! Thirty-seven views since lunch." Three of them were from new followers. My latest episode, "The ABCs of Poisoning," was going viral!

SNIPER93 said: Loved the quiz at the end where I got to test my diagnostic skills.

That was my 8th grade Science teacher, a dedicated fan of my web show who also supported arming teachers with assault rifles as a way to end school violence. I couldn't say I agree with him on the topic, but I liked his moxie.

AutopsyAl asked: What's the difference between arsenic poisoning and food poisoning?

I closed my eyes and shook my head. AutopsyAl, the poor guy, came up with some ridiculous questions. He didn't limit them to my forensic videos. Once he asked me how to tell the difference between a vampire bite and a dog bite. Still, he had been following me loyally for years, so I'd answer his poisoning question later when I had time to explain it in terms he could understand.

I scrolled down. GirlofSteel had written back: No, you imbecile! The murder happened ages ago.

Dillon the Villain didn't know words like "imbecile," or where to accurately place a comma. Was GirlofSteel for real?

I messaged back: Need name of victim, date, and location. Anything you know.

"Please, please, please be a real person, with a real crime to investigate," I whispered as I hit "send."

WHEN I GOT HOME, I took the steps two at a time, stuck my head in the back door and called out to Grandpa. "I'm home, but I'm going down to the vacant lot to throw my boomerang for a while."

Chaucer, my hundred-pound bloodhound, wagged himself to the door. I gave him a quick ear rub. "Hey buddy, I'll be back soon. Keep an eye on Grandpa."

He whined, letting me know he wanted to go along. "Sorry boy. I'll take you next time." He raised his head, howled, then tried to stare me into submission with his droopy brown eyes.

"I'll tell you what—we'll compromise."

I ran into my bedroom, grabbed a dirty sock, and held it to his nose.

"Take a big whiff."

I pulled it away. "Now stay here, and no peeking." Sometimes he peeked.

In the backyard, I hid the sock, then turned Chaucer loose. "Find the sock!"

He dashed out the back door while I grabbed my boomerang and let the screen door slam behind me.

I pedaled my bike down Bending Oak Drive in the shade of the ancient oaks, glad that summer was finally here. No more school meant there would be no reason for Mom to deliver one of her lectures. Her favorites were: "Don't Argue with Adults, Even When They're Wrong" and "Just Try a Little Harder to Fit In."

Mom didn't get it. I was a black jelly bean, everyone's least favorite flavor. She gave me pep talks all the time, as if I could miraculously turn into a red jelly bean simply by identifying as one. It didn't work that way. I was a prisoner of my own black licorice life.

Still, when Mom lectured me about trying harder to make friends, I told her I would. I'd been lying about that for years. It's nearly impossible to say "no" to your single mom when she offers to buy you an obscenely overpriced shirt from the mall so you'd "fit in."

My peer assimilation problems went deeper than clothes.

Even trickier is how to explain that I'm not interested in fitting in, or mall clothes, but I'd be willing to go to a *freakin' school dance* if she'd buy me a ground-penetrating radar detector. That's a hard sell.

As I cruised down the hill, purposely hitting the lumps and cracks in the pavement, I spotted a moving truck at the old Johnson place, across the street from the vacant lot.

The Johnsons died in a car accident when I was little. Their house was empty for years. Time, neglect, and hurricanes had almost destroyed it. Most of the windows were broken, and the roof had more holes than shingles. Rumors about why it had been empty so long included everything from toxic levels of radon to its history as a group home for criminally-insane kids. Mom said none of that was true, and that it never sold because it had orange countertops, green shag carpet, and a rodent problem.

I didn't follow the real estate market like I used to, but I knew someone had bought the house when I was in seventh grade, torn it down to the foundation, and started over. The new house looked like something out of a fancy architecture magazine.

I leaned my bike against the massive oak in the vacant lot and wished that a kid my age with a love of forensic science and boomerangs was moving in. If he disliked the humans as much as I did, then officially, I'd hit the trifecta.

I didn't know why I bothered, except that I could picture the smile on Mom's face if I made an actual friend. For once she'd feel like a good mom, and not the parent of the weird kid that nobody liked.

I limbered up and positioned myself for a trick catch I'd been working on. Just as the boomerang flew from my hands, I heard a little girl squeal.

"Look, Hannah, our bikes are off. Let's go for a ride!"

I turned toward the voice to see movers pushing three kids' bikes across the driveway.

"Josey, we can't. Mom's only giving us a ten-minute break from the boxes."

The dark-haired little girl whined and walked back in the garage, but the older one looked in my direction and yelled, "Dude! Look out!" I turned in time to *almost* prevent my boomerang from nailing me in the gut.

Oomph! I doubled over.

She crossed the street.

"What was that?"

I tried to hide my humiliation as I picked up my boomerang. "Nothing."

"A boomerang?" She snickered at my hand-made Baltic birch weapon. "You got attacked by a boomerang! Isn't that like the official sport of the friendless or something?"

I held it in one hand and grabbed my bike with the other.

"Wait, you're leaving? It was a joke. Get it? You don't need a friend to play with a boomerang because it comes back to you."

I wasn't going to answer. I would let my exit speak for itself. The back of my head and the way I didn't turn around would tell her exactly what I thought of her so-called joke.

"Where are you going?" she asked.

I showed her my angry back.

"Don't leave! It was funny."

Then she took an exaggerated sniff of the air and said, "God! What is that smell? It's like rotting cat!"

I rolled my eyes. *It's sulfur from the salt marsh—the smell of summer, the perfume of freedom, you annoying little...*

I didn't finish the sentence in my head because Dr. B said I should clean up my mental monologue and have more positive thoughts.

I would get right on that once I had slain Dillon Buckley,

ended world hunger, balanced the federal budget, and finished *War and Peace*.

I got on my bike.

The girl called after me, "But wait. I just…"

"Whatever!" I mumbled as I pedaled off the grass, and onto the road. So much for the trifecta.

2

In 2003, authorities charged Felix Freed with first-degree murder. He was an elderly man with dementia, who suffocated his 90-year-old nursing home neighbor. Freed could not explain why he killed his friend. After spending a year in the local jail and two years in a hospital for the criminally insane, prosecutors dropped the charges. The legal community continues to struggle with how to handle criminals with dementia. See episode 27 of **Forensics 411** *"I Don't Recall."*

I RETURNED home to find Chaucer lying on the back porch thumping his tail against the deck with my sock tucked under his chin.

"You are such a good boy! Yes, you are!"

He stood up and wagged.

"Let's go get you a treat."

Chaucer followed me into the kitchen and sat in front of the pantry where I kept his dog cookies. After rewarding him, I called to Grandpa, "I'm back."

"Can you make me some soup?" Grandpa asked from the den. "I'm freezing."

It was 88 degrees outside, but the house was glacial. I went from room to room checking the window units. I think we were the only people in North Carolina without central air. I adjusted each thermostat, then went to the den. "Grandpa, you had every air conditioner set on 55 degrees. You've got to leave them where Mom sets them, okay?"

"It's my house! Why should Angela control the temperature?"

Because you end up freezing in June, that's why.

Doctors diagnosed Grandpa's dementia when I was in sixth grade. Mom didn't like him to use the stove because she worried that he might forget to turn it off and burn the house down. That's why *I* had to make him soup.

I didn't think Grandpa was that far gone. *Yet.* But I dreaded the inevitable day when he would no longer recognize us. He was the closest thing I had to a dad, and I didn't want to imagine what it would be like without him. I'd already lost one father.

Not that I ever *had* him.

While the soup heated, I gave Chaucer a proper greeting. "You're getting so good at finding things. Pretty soon I'm going to start burying stuff, then we'll really test that nose!"

"That dog's sniffer doesn't work for crap," Grandpa grumbled.

"It's perfect," I said, scratching Chaucer's ears.

"Worst huntin' dog I ever had!" Grandpa said as he moseyed into the kitchen.

He pointed to the kitchen table. "Have a seat boy. Use those people skills you been learning with that headshrinker." He nibbled on some crackers. "Back in my day you didn't have to go to a doctor to learn how to talk to people, and you didn't have to take medicine to make you sit still or be happy. We didn't have to wear helmets to ride a bicycle, and nobody was allergic to peanuts. We ate them by the pound." He shook his head in disgust."You kids today are mollycoddled!"

"Uh-huh." I nodded, not in the mood to argue with him about my so-called pampered life.

"Anything interesting happen at school today?"

"It was the last day. That's always good. Oh, and somebody's moving into the abandoned house."

"Which one?"

There was only one abandoned house in our neighborhood, but it made Grandpa mad when you reminded him of things he'd forgotten. "102 Bending Oak," I answered. "They pretty much tore the old one down." I set the bowl of soup in front of him.

Grandpa slurped and nodded. "Where the McFarlands used to live?"

"No, the house where that old couple, the Johnsons, lived. The ones that died in a car accident."

"*Before* them, the McFarlands lived there. Things happened around here before you were born, you know." He shook his head, "I thought your mama said you were gifted."

"I am."

"The McFarlands built that house back in the seventies," Grandpa said. "It was the first one on the street after ours. In fact, there wasn't even a paved road when your grandma and I built this house. The McFarlands were good people, but I can't blame them for moving away after what happened to their daughter."

I sat up straight. "What happened?"

"It was years ago, back in the eighties. The parents, Mike and Connie, went out of town and left the girl at home alone. I think her name was Stacy. I *know* she rode bus 240. They came home the next day, and she was gone. The house had been robbed, and no one ever saw that girl again."

Because of his dementia, Grandpa couldn't remember what he'd eaten for lunch, but he could tell you the names and addresses of every kid who ever rode the bus while he was the transportation coordinator for the school system. Dementia was weird... and cruel.

"How come you've never told me about this? You know how much I love crime."

"I wouldn't go around advertising that," Grandpa said. "The kids already think you're weird because of those movies you make."

"They're not movies—it's a web show about forensics. I have hundreds of followers." Soon to be thousands.

"Followers aren't friends," Grandpa said. "You need some friends like a normal kid. Life isn't a solo sport." He curled his lip. "Well, you need *one* friend. That's all. My best friend was a fella named Vince, we used to…"

I zoned out, imagining the scenarios that could've led to the McFarland girl's disappearance. Was she kidnapped? Murdered? Did she run away or drown in the waterway? Was she chained up in someone's basement?

"…they used to hire kids to take the census back then," Grandpa was saying, leaving me to wonder what on earth I had missed.

"So, the girl's name was Stacy McFarland, and she disappeared when Mom was a kid?"

"Yep. She babysat your mom a few times. After the girl went missing, the family fell apart. The brother got messed up on drugs. Mike and Connie divorced and sold the house to the Johnsons, but even then, it took a few years to sell." He shook his head. "Nobody wants to buy a house with that kind of history. The Johnsons lived there for a good bit, then they got killed on the way home from church. That house is cursed!"

Since Grandpa's memory was clinically less-than-reliable, I'd have to do some research. "They have *no idea* what happened to her?" I asked. "She just disappeared into thin air—defying all laws of physics?"

He gazed out the window for a second. "Well, Buckley said she ran away, but he's nuttier than a squirrel turd."

"Buckley" was Chester Buckley, the police chief, and Dillon's great-uncle. Vista Point had Buckleys slithering out from every rock. Dillon's grandfather was the mayor, and his dad and uncle ran the Ford dealership. Dillon thought that made him important.

I got up. With a name and a time period, I'd research the case. It could make a great *Forensics 411* episode. Despite the arrival of the mean girl, the summer looked promising.

3

According to a study by economists released in 2009, there is a link between a person's name and the likelihood that they will commit a crime. The more uncommon the name, the more likely a person is to end up in jail. See **Forensics 411** episode 36, "What's in a Name?" featuring convicted offenders, Crystal Metheny, Bud Weisser, Sirloin Duffy, Joseph Moron, Edward Cocaine, Draco Slaughter and Lancelot Superbad, just to name a few.

LATER THAT EVENING, when the sun was sneaking behind the pines, I went back to the vacant lot to throw my boomerang. It was the only wide-open space in the neighborhood large enough to accommodate my skills. No way was the repellent new girl going to strong-arm me out of my favorite hobby. At least temporarily, she was less popular than me. I had the advantage.

My grandpa gave me my first boomerang when I was five. I loved it so much I begged Mom to change my name from Henry to Boomerang. After negotiations, we compromised on Boomer as a nickname. Since I was about to start high school, I thought it would be a good time for another name change, but what name would set me up for the most success in high school? Henry? Harry? H-Dog? Josh?

I took a deep breath and felt a sense of satisfaction as I raised my arm for the second throw of summer. I released it at a forty-five-degree angle to the breeze and watched it circle back to me, spinning against the orange and pink sunset. With perfect timing, I caught it behind my back.

I heard clapping and turned toward the noise. There was Mean-Girl, watching me. Without warning, she waved.

No one ever waved at me, especially with all five fingers. Usually, they just used the middle one, and it wasn't meant as a greeting. After proving herself as an enemy of the state, waving made no sense.

While I considered her five-finger-wave, she walked to the end of her driveway and called out, "I'm sorry. Did I confuse you with the hand gesture? It's customary in most western societies that when a person waves at you, you wave back."

I squeezed the foam inside my pocket and didn't respond. Dr. B always says "don't engage."

She reached my side of the street and thrust her hand at me. "So, we kind of got off to a less-than-ideal start earlier. Sorry about that. I'm Hannah. As you know, I just moved in." She pointed to her house with the hand that was not invading my personal space.

I looked at her hand, and she looked at me. Our eyes narrowed on each other as if waiting for the other to take three paces and reach for their gun. I palmed my boomerang, ready to defend myself.

She surveyed me up and down. "It looks like you're all healed up from the attack, and you and your boomerang have made nice." She tried to hold eye contact, but I wouldn't allow it.

"About now is when you tell me *your* name. And my hand's sticking out because you're supposed to shake it. At least that's how we did things in Pittsburgh." She smacked her lips. "Aren't Southerners supposed to be friendly?"

I surprised myself by moving my hand forward and projectile-vomiting my name, "Boomer. Boomer Boyd." At once, I wished I'd told her my name was Josh... or Lancelot Superbad. Every guy named Josh was cool, and nobody messed with a guy named Superbad.

"Boomer? Is that a nickname?"

I held up my boomerang as explanation. I was spent from the handshake. She released my hand, and I wiped it on my shorts, not sure how to proceed.

She put her hands on her hips. "Okay, let me rephrase the question. What's your real name?"

I looked over my shoulder to see if anyone from school was hiding. This encounter had all the characteristics of a Dillon-orchestrated set-up. He was dumb, but not dumb enough. He didn't usually miss an opportunity to enlist an unwitting stranger in one of his plots.

When I didn't answer, she threw her hands in the air. "You know what? Forget it! I'm new here and don't know anyone. I'm trying to be nice, but you're giving me nothing to work with. So, see you later." She stepped off the curb.

I stood frozen. Then I heard my mom's voice say *try a little harder*, followed by my shrink saying, *make eye contact*.

For them, and them alone, I forced myself to look at her nose, which was a little too big for her face, but not so big that it made her ugly. Freckles were sprinkled across it. She had sandy blond, curly hair pulled back in a tight ponytail. Her eyes were a haunting hazel that reminded me of a cat.

I hated cats.

"Well, thanks for being so friendly. My parents would've been positively giddy if they thought I'd met someone." She glared at me with those eyes that held me against my will. "I'll go talk to the voices in my head. At least they talk back."

"Are you schizophrenic?" I asked.

"What?" She pivoted to face me.

"Schizophrenic. David Berkowitz is schizophrenic. He's my favorite serial killer, well, one of them."

"You have a favorite serial killer?" She tucked a frizzy piece of hair back into her ponytail. "That's... weird."

"He's not my *favorite*, but he's in my top ten," I answered. "I know it's cliché, but Charles Manson is my number one. He was the consummate psychopath." I smiled just thinking about the complexity of Manson's disturbed life. I could only hope to investigate a killer like Manson during my career at the FBI.

She studied her black, chipped fingernail polish. "I guess I'd go with John Wayne Gacy. He had that whole dressing-like-a-clown-thing. Nothing's creepier than clowns. But I'm also fascinated by Henry Louis Wallace. You never hear much about African-American serial killers. That's not really fair."

"You're right. I sometimes forget about him. Wallace killed a bunch of women right here in North Carolina back in the 1990s." I made a mental note to research minority serial killers for a *Forensics 411* episode. Crazy white guys shouldn't get all the attention.

"My name's actually Henry Boyd, but for as long as I can remember people have called me 'Boomer,' because of my exceptional boomeranging skills."

"Exceptional is debatable." She smirked. "So, what do you want me to call you?"

I thought hard, stood tall and said, "Hank." It had a sturdy, old-Western-movie feel to it, and could be the beginning of a new era for me.

She examined me from feet to head. "You don't look like a Hank."

"I don't?" I asked, shrinking a couple inches.

"No, but I'll roll with it," she said. "I'm going to be a freshman. What about you?"

Seeking courage, I squished the foam inside my pocket and said, "Same."

"Do you live around here?" she asked.

"Up the street." I pointed north and then looked down at the roadside where my feet had made troughs in the dirt.

"Maybe you could show me around and introduce me to the other kids our age?"

Doubtful. Taking Hannah door-to-door to meet the mouth-breathers would not go without consequence. There's no telling what a kid from school would do if I came a-knocking at their door with a girl in tow. At the minimum, I'd get the door slammed in my face, assuming someone answered it to begin with. At worst, I'd get the crap beat out of me. Mom preferred I avoid physical confrontations whenever possible, and I tried to oblige.

I considered this new girl with a favorite serial killer. Instead of handing her over to the popular crowd, I could keep her for myself. She had a bit of a problem with first impressions anyway. I could use that to my advantage. Here was someone who knew me *but not anybody else* in Vista Point. All I had to do was keep it that way. In no time, we'd be friends.

"Hank?" she said, tilting her head. When I didn't answer, she said it more insistently.

"Huh?"

"So, can you show me around the neighborhood tomorrow—maybe about eleven?"

I waited for a sinister laugh, but it didn't come.

"Sure."

"Awesome!" She smiled a sparkly, braces-filled smile, and pushed a springy curl from her forehead. "That'll be great."

She pointed toward her house. "Now, I'm going to walk back across the street. Before I go into the house, I'll stop to wave at you. You know what to do in response, right?"

I nodded slowly as she floated away.

As promised, she turned back just before entering the garage and waved a real, five-fingered wave. In return, I saluted her with my boomerang.

She called out, "Meh, keep working on it. More hand, less boomerang!" She waved again and yelled, "See you tomorrow."

After she disappeared into the house, I tossed my boomerang in the air triumphantly. I might've just made one of those things called a friend!

4

The sense of smell is the strongest of the five senses in both dogs and humans. A Bloodhound's sense of smell is so reliable that prosecutors have used it as testimony in court. The trickiest part of the testimony is phrasing all questions as "yes/no" since most Blood-hounds are not conversationalists. See Forensics 411 *episode 6, "Sniffing Out Crime."*

THE NEXT MORNING, I woke early to find Chaucer perched beside my bed, his chin resting on the mattress. I rubbed his long velvety ears while I checked *Forensics 411* on my phone. "Yes! Another 67 views and six new followers."

I kicked my legs over the side of the bed. "Come on, let's get you something to eat." He cut in front of me, heading to the pantry. I scooped out a heaping cup of kibble while he turned circles of excitement.

Grandpa yelled from the den, "I already fed that good-for-nothing dog!"

"Chaucer told me he's starving," I called back.

"There's a reason his nose's that long. That dog's a filthy liar!"

Chaucer jumped up and slobbered all over my face to let me know that he was nothing but truthful.

I whispered, "I know, boy. We can't trust that old Grandpa to remember if he fed you or not."

I dumped the dog food in his bowl. Chaucer dove in as I retreated to the bathroom to prepare for what could be a life-changing day.

I EXAMINED the face in the mirror.

If a witness were describing me to a police sketch artist, he would say I was tall for my age, skinny, had a long nose, narrow face, and brown eyes with thick brows. And a dimple—just one —in my left cheek.

My skin was dark considering my grandpa's Scottish heritage and my fair, red-headed mom. Logic and biology told me my complexion came from my father. But other than his skin tone, I didn't know anything about him—not even his name.

I ran my hands over buzz-cut hair. I'd worn it that way since second grade when Dillon first weaponized gum.

I told the boy in the mirror, "Today could change your life. Don't be a know-it-all. You know what Mom says about that. When in doubt, remain silent. But also, be tough. If she starts giving you crap, just leave."

Reminding yourself how to act is what Dr. B calls "self-talk." He thinks it can solve almost anything. So, I chatted myself up while I used Mom's tweezers to prune my uni-brow. They called it "man-scaping" in Mom's magazines.

I practiced some of the non-verbal communications that Dr. B and I had been working on: the "interested nod" was my latest. Even if someone is boring or stupid, you're supposed to fake being interested in what they say. Dr. B calls it "people skills."

I advised my reflection. "Smile, so she notices your dimple. Mom says it's adorable."

After I had made myself look as good as I could, I went into the kitchen and poured a bowl of cereal.

Mom was coming in from outside with sweat dripping down her face.

"Hi Sweetie," she said, patting her face with a napkin. "You're up and dressed early for the first day of summer vacation."

She sniffed the air. "Are you wearing cologne?"

I grabbed a dishtowel from the counter and wiped my neck. "No."

As I carried my cereal across the kitchen, Mom asked, "Why didn't you sleep in?"

I sat down.

"Got plans," I answered, then shoveled a spoonful of cereal into my mouth.

"What kind of plans?"

I finished chewing, swallowed hard, then said, "Meeting a friend" as casually as possible.

As expected, she pounced. "A friend? What kind of friend? Where's he from? Have you met his family? Do you know his last name?"

Last time I made a "friend," I didn't get his last name, which proved problematic. Mom would say disastrous.

I rolled my eyes. "It's not a big deal. Her name is Hannah. She moved into the new house on the lot where the Johnsons used to live. She's from Pennsylvania."

"It's a girl?"

"Don't make a big deal out of it."

Mom looked out the window. "Should I call her parents?"

"No! You can't!" I waved my arms around for emphasis. "*Please*, promise you won't. That would be so humiliating."

"But remember what happened in sixth—"

I raised my hand to cut her off.

"It's okay. I'll have my cell phone." The presence of a cell phone was inexplicably reassuring to parents, as if it formed a protective force-field around their kid. I got mine a little too late for that.

"Okay, but get her last name and text it to me," Mom said.

"No probs, Mom."

5

In the art of distraction, the distracter manages an object or action, so the other person notices said object. By contrast, when you misdirect a person, you more deliberately direct the person's attention to, or from, an object or action. See Forensics 411 *episode 20, "Made You Look."*

THAT MORNING GIRLOFSTEEL had still not replied to my private message.

In the front yard, I discovered the cause of mom's sweaty, discombobulated kitchen face. Soggy toilet paper hung from the highest limbs of our trees and filled the trash can under the porch.

I shut my eyes and tried to slow my breathing. How many times over the years had I awoken to find our trees draped in triple-ply excrement eraser and cleaned it up before Mom could see it? *Had she been doing the same thing? Were both of us trying to protect the other from the same unpleasant truth?*

I SLAMMED the trash lid shut and hit the road. While I biked, I contemplated who GirlofSteel might be. Did she identify with steel because of its strength, or was she a wordsmith whose screen name referred to "steel" as a verb, which meant to mentally prepare oneself to face something difficult?

I stopped at the end of Hannah's driveway and peeked in her mailbox. There were two letters forwarded from an address in Pittsburgh, to John Simmons. Assuming John Simmons was her father, I texted Mom: Hannah's last name is Simmons.

At 10:54 I knocked on her front door, armed with what I considered a flawless plan of misdirection to avoid having to introduce her to the kids in the neighborhood. We got on our bikes, and I led her out the neighborhood entrance.

As we pedaled, I tried to steal glances at Hannah. In the light of day, her hair was a dark blond nest of curls. She had it pulled back in a ponytail again, but it was clear that if she released it from its elastic incarceration, things could get crazy.

"I thought you were going to give me a tour of the neighborhood," Hannah said as we pedaled up the state road that served as the main thoroughfare of Vista Point.

"That's boring," I explained with authority. I had self-talked my way into a state of confidence before knocking on her front door. I babbled over the sound of the cars that rushed past us. "Our neighborhood has a pool, a bunch of houses and lots of big, old trees. Your house and my house are on the Intracoastal Waterway, which is the old part of the neighborhood. The houses closest to the highway are newer. That's all there is to know."

I turned onto Fripp Road, and the sound of cars disappeared. A damp aroma of mossy salt air replaced the smell of vehicle exhaust. Large live oaks draped with Spanish moss formed a canopy that blocked the sky and immediately lowered the temperature by ten degrees. I sighed.

Hannah looked up at the arching branches of the immense trees. "Wow. This is beautiful!"

So far, so good. She'd already forgotten about the neighborhood tour. "This isn't our final destination, but it's nice, isn't it?" I pointed ahead to where sunlight reappeared at the end of the tree tunnel. "That's where we're headed."

On the other side of the tunnel, the crown of oaks gave way to the North Carolina sunshine. Straight ahead was the Intracoastal Waterway. "That's Fripp's Marina." I motioned to a cinderblock building that advertised live bait and cold beer. I pointed to the left. "But this is why we're here."

Hannah's preternatural eyes widened. "What is it?"

"It's Fripp's Boatyard," I answered. "But people call it Fripp's Graveyard because boats come here to die."

The field hosted hundreds of boats. Some were too big for dry dock. Others awaited repairs. Owners abandoned the rest. I didn't understand how someone could leave such beautiful boats to bake, rust and decay in the field of weeds.

We propped our bikes against the chain-link fence, and I led her through the gate guarded by a faded "No Trespassing" sign pocked by BB gun pellets.

Hannah stopped and pointed at the sign, "I don't think we're supposed to go in here."

"It's okay. That sign doesn't mean us. Old Man Fripp just doesn't want people back here stealing stuff from the boats. We're not gonna do that."

"Are you sure?"

"Positive," I answered. "I have not planned a robbery for us this morning."

Sounds whirled from the repair shop on the opposite end of the boatyard. Hannah pointed to a forty-foot sailboat whose keel was taller than many of the other boats.

"Wow! I never realized sailboats had all those parts under the water. We don't get many sailboats in Pittsburgh."

Giant tripod-looking things supported the boat along each side. Boaters called it blocking.

She jogged ahead of me. "Look at the corny names. *Knotty Girl*," she said motioning to an old day-cruiser that lay tilted, almost on its side, at one corner of the boatyard. It was overgrown with kudzu. "Oh, brother, check that out," she pointed to a cracked and peeling trawler named *2BOrNaut2Be*. She clicked her tongue, moving quickly among the boats. "Boaters must like puns."

"Yeah," I answered.

"Do you have a boat?" she asked.

"Not a big one. Mine's about the size of a pick-up truck. I keep it tied to the dock behind my house. It used to be my Grandpa's but Mom doesn't let him use it anymore since he got sick."

"What's wrong with him?"

"He has dementia." I'd never told anyone that before.

"Oh, I'm sorry," Hannah said.

"Thanks," I whispered.

We continued walking between the abandoned boats. "What's your boat's name?"

"Um… *Crime Cat*."

"Is that a pun?"

"Yeah. It's a catamaran, and I'm into forensics," I answered. "You know, the study of crime, DNA, blood splatter patterns, forensic odontology, stuff like that. It's a hobby mostly, but someday I'm going to win the Nobel prize for forensics."

"They give a Nobel in forensics?" she asked, cocking her head to the side.

"Not yet, but they will once they hear about *me*," I answered proudly.

"So…" she said as she took her phone from her pocket. "Maybe you can help me?"

She typed something into the phone, then held it up. "I sent a message to this guy I found online because I have some suspicions about our house. He's some detective from a webshow called *Forensics 411*. He messaged me back but wanted details about where I lived and stuff. I got a cringy feeling that he might be a creeper, so I haven't answered him."

My heart jumped in the best way possible. "You're `GirlofSteel`?"

"How do you know my screen name?" Her eyes narrowed. "Do you follow this *Forensics 411* detective guy?"

"I *am* that *Forensics 411* detective guy!"

"No way," she said. "I mean, I didn't know. You never show your face on the web show." Her eyes got wide. "So, you're like a local celebrity?"

Local celebrity? Interesting idea.

"Umm, you could say that." Of course, my type of celebrity was more infamy than fame. But *she* didn't know that the paparazzi I dealt with were kids armed with cell phones videoing Dillon Buckley being "so cool" and "hilarious" to me, which amounted to him being a moron.

Her forehead crinkled between her eyes. "So, you're probably Mr. Popularity at school."

Was that a question?

I stood as straight as I could and lied my butt right off. "Well, I don't like to brag…" I flashed a grin that would put my dimple on full display.

She nodded and smiled. "And modest too. I like that."

It wasn't really a lie. Dr. Blanchard said there was an art to knowing when to tell the truth and when to protect someone's feelings. Couldn't I lie to protect my own feelings?

"I liked your rap about the Automated Fingerprint Identification System, especially when you rhymed fingerprint with Rupert Grint."

"That's one of my favorites, too," I answered proudly, feeling buoyed by new-found celebrity. "My latest episode is about poisoning. You should check it out."

"Definitely," she answered. "Since you're the detective from *Forensics 411* and live in Vista Point, you probably know what happened at the old house that my parents tore down—right?"

"I've done a bit of research"—if that's what you called questioning my addled grandfather. "I don't think there was a murder there."

She shook her head. "After my parents bought the house, I heard them whispering. Mom said something like 'I don't think we should tell the kids about it. It might scare them.' And then another time I heard her tell my father that she was glad they were tearing the old house down, in case it was haunted. I looked up the address of the house online, but all I could find were real estate listings. The house was for sale for a really long time."

"Years," I answered as we walked among the old boats. "The couple that used to live there was killed in a car accident, and they didn't have any kids, so the bank took it over."

"Yeah, my parents got it as a foreclosure. That's why they were able to tear it down and start over. They didn't like the house, but they loved the location right on the water."

"Maybe your parents were just talking about the Johnsons dying?" I said.

"I don't think so. It was just the way Mom said it. My gut tells me that the old house had a secret."

She raised an eyebrow. "Would you be interested in doing some investigating?"

"Um, sure," I answered smoothly, while inside I was celebrating. A girl... a smart, mostly nice girl wanted to spend time with me.

Me!

I could've told her what Grandpa had told me, but if his story ended up being wrong, I'd look stupid. I'd already looked like an idiot in front of her with my boomerang. No way would I give Hannah any reason to suspect that I was anything other than Hank, the coolest local celebrity in town.

"Great! I plan on being a writer so the research would be good practice."

"What kind of writer?" I asked.

"Anything but poetry and plays. Right now, I'm working on

a story about Jewish kids from Transylvania sent to Auschwitz during the Holocaust. It turns out they're all vampires, and they take over the concentration camp, destroy the Third Reich, and prevent millions of other Jews from dying. It's sort of an alternative-history-paranormal-fantasy-adventure."

She smiled proudly.

I used my *I find what you're saying interesting* nod. "Sounds like a best seller."

When Hannah started complaining about the heat, we got on our bikes and headed home.

While we were in the shade of the tree tunnel, she said, "I'm going to be on the community swim team, and I've got to go sign up this afternoon. Maybe we could hang out tomorrow and get started on the investigation?"

"Yeah… I guess so… I mean if you want to." Again, the internal celebration. My mental monologue had never been so positive.

We pedaled in silence until we got back in the neighborhood.

"I'm not sure what time practice will be, but I'll stop by your house afterward."

"Sure," I answered, playing it cool. After I'd given her my address, I stood at the intersection with my bike and watched her ride away.

At that point, I planned to endear myself to Hannah so that by the end of the summer we'd be inseparable. The best way to maximize my time with her, and subsequently lure her into the trappings of my under-appreciated-yet-magnetic-personality, was through forensics. She already thought I was a celebrity. I could work with that!

6

The first step in gathering evidence is finding it. The criminologist must document everything at the crime scene, in writing, and in photos, as it can be difficult to know at the beginning of an investigation what is important. For more information see Forensics 411 *episode 9, "Things Aren't Always What They Seem."*

As PROMISED, Hannah showed up at my house the next day.

Grandpa answered the door.

"Is Hank here?" she asked.

When I heard her voice, I dropped the broom I'd been using in the kitchen and ran to the door.

"Frank?" Grandpa asked. "Who the hell's Frank?"

"Hank," Hannah said cautiously. She wore a swim team t-shirt, and her curly hair was weighed down with water.

"I don't know anybody named Hank," he answered.

"That's me," I said, wanting to get Grandpa, dressed in his favorite kilt, away from Hannah.

He looked confused. "When'd you start going by 'Hank'?"

I laughed. "Good one, Grandpa," I said, turning him around toward the kitchen. I whispered, "A couple of days ago."

He spun back around. "Well, that's gonna confuse the crap out of me. You know I'm already losin' my mind!"

"You can still call me 'Boomer.'"

He wrinkled his nose. "Well fine, Boomer-Hank, or whatever-your-name-is, this girl's here for you."

He surveyed Hannah. "Why're you all wet?"

"Um, just came from swim practice."

He grunted and turned to go back into the den, but then circled back to face us. "Just so you know, this is a kilt, not a skirt. Lots of people get confused about that because they don't have any culture."

"Oh," Hannah answered, turning as red as Grandpa's tartan. "It's lovely."

"I'm a direct descendant of the Boyd Clan of Ayrshire," Grandpa declared. "Now don't be too loud, *The Price is Right* is on, and it's almost time for the showcase showdown."

"See ya, Grandpa," I said.

After seeing Hannah's house, I preferred she not see mine up-close. The outside was more like a cabin than a house, and I don't think that the linoleum-made-to-look-like-bricks fooled anyone. Throw in our furniture that was as scratchy as it was plaid, and it was better to spend our time outdoors. "Let's go outside," I suggested. "I'll show you my boat."

We walked to the back deck where my bloodhound was basking in the sun. He scrambled to a standing position when he saw us. "This is Chaucer."

"Oh my gosh, he's so cute!" she said, as she tousled his ears.

He liked that a lot, so he jumped up and put his paws on her shoulders.

"Be careful, boy!" I said, trying to grab him by the collar and pull him off. "He thinks he's a lap dog."

"Oh no, don't," she said patting his head. "I used to have a St. Bernard. I love big dogs. Mozart died two years ago. He was the only dog I've ever had."

"Mozart?" I raised an eyebrow to make myself look inquisitive.

Hannah blushed. "I had just seen all the *Beethoven* movies right before we got him. I thought I was being clever." She giggled. "Tchaikovsky was way too hard to spell."

Chaucer released his paws from her shoulders, but she bent down and wrapped her arms around his neck again. "He's perfect!"

"Sorry about Mozart."

I couldn't imagine what I would do if something happened to Chaucer. He'd been my best friend since I got him in sixth grade.

I pointed down the slope of our backyard. "The dock's this way. Watch where you walk, he loves to dig holes, but he doesn't fill them back in."

When we got to the dock, I said, "This is *Crime Cat*. She's a classic," which was a euphemism for old.

"Can we go for a ride?" she asked.

"Sure." I looked up at the sky. "But we need to hurry. It's gonna rain soon."

"It's barely cloudy."

"It will be. Trust me, I'm a pluviophile."

"A what?"

"A pluviophile. It's a person interested in rain."

Hannah scoffed. "You must really have to fight the girls off with all your unusual hobbies. Are you a mathlete, too?"

"Um, maybe," I mumbled.

"Just kidding." She patted my arm.

I flinched slightly.

"I respect the trappings of nerdery," she said. "What was that word? Pluviophile?"

I nodded.

"I'm going to remember that. I try to learn a new word every day. 'Pluviophile' will be today's word-of-the-day. That's much better than yesterday's word, 'concatenate.' That means—"

"To link together!" I said.

"How'd you know that?"

"I read a lot." People don't feel sorry for you if you're sitting alone reading. That's normal, like boomeranging.

"Me, too."

As we motored to her house, the dark clouds rolled in from the ocean. While I tied the boat to her decaying dock, we heard rumbles of thunder and crossed her yard in a run as the large first drops of rain began falling.

Her mom was standing in the kitchen chopping vegetables. "Hi."

"Mom, this is Hank. Can he hang out for a little bit?"

Mrs. Simmons smiled. "Hi, Hank. Of course, you can hang out. Do you live around here?"

Mrs. Simmons had white, springy curls, that made me think of a Norse goddess. Aside from Hannah's darker complexion, they looked a lot alike.

"I live up the street," I answered.

"And what grade are you going to be in?"

"Ninth, Mom," Hannah answered impatiently. "He's gonna be in ninth just like me. He's got a boat, likes to read, plays with a boomerang, he lives with his grandfather, and Charles Manson is his favorite serial killer."

"Oh," Mrs. Simmons said, her eyebrows pinched together. "Well, I'm more of a Bundy girl myself."

"Many women were!"

Hannah positioned her hands on her hips. "Enough with the interrogation," she told her mother. "We gotta go."

"Fine," Mrs. Simmons answered. "Just remember you're supposed to get those boxes unpacked. I want this place to start to feel like home."

Hannah gave me a nudge in the ribs and said, "My room's that way." As we walked past her mom, I heard Mrs. Simmons whisper, "See, I told you things would be different here."

HANNAH LED ME UPSTAIRS. My legs trembled a bit as I made my first trip into a girl's bedroom.

It was triple the size of mine, with furniture that actually matched. There was a large bay window that faced the waterway and ocean, and a set of doors opened out onto her very own balcony. It looked nothing like how I pictured a girl's room: no unicorns or rainbows. There were some posters already hanging on one wall: *The Fault in Our Stars; Me, Earl, and the Dying Girl;* and *13 Reasons Why.*

That's some uplifting chick-lit!

On the opposite wall hung Beyoncé and Lady Gaga.

She didn't have puke green carpet, 1970s fake paneling, or a wheezing window air conditioner. Her family had central air and all that came with it.

"You want to help?" she asked as she dragged a box toward her walk-in closet.

"Sure," I answered, knowing I could learn a lot about her by combing through her personal things.

"That's mostly books and stuff that goes on my shelves over there," she pointed. "There are some scissors on my bed."

I faced her windows so I could enjoy the sound of the pelting rain and got to work. About halfway through the first box, my hands stopped shaking. I found a yearbook from Millview Elementary School that was a few years old. Just inside the front cover was a letter written on stationery decorated with school buses and chalkboards. It said, "From the Desk of Mrs. Franklin." I glanced toward the closet to make sure Hannah was still in there, then started reading.

Dear Hannah,

I know this has been a hard year for you. Your classmates and I are praying for you and your family. We signed this yearbook with the hope that in the future you might be able to look back and recall some of

the good things that happened during fifth grade. We hope to see you
back at school soon. Until that time comes, we wish you all the best.
    Sincerely,
    Mrs. Franklin

"So, Hank," Hannah called from deep inside the closet.

I panicked, remembering that *I* was Hank, shoved the year-book between some books on the shelf, and turned to see her standing in the doorway of her closet.

"Should I wear my hair like this on the first day of school?" She had released her mane from its ponytail, and it had expanded to the width of the doorway.

I swallowed hard and lied just like Dr. Blanchard taught me. "Um... that looks great." In reality, it looked like the nest the ospreys built down on the channel marker behind our house.

Her eyes got big. "I'm rocking this look, right?"

I gave her my *I find what you're saying interesting* look.

"Dude, I was kidding. I'm like Medusa. I've always had curls, but this humidity is going to be the death of me." She stared off into space for a second then said, "Do you think I could get a doctor's note to wear a hat all the time?"

"I'm not sure having a bad hair day is considered a medical condition."

"Since moving here, it's a bad hair *life*," she said. "You have no idea how vicious girls our age can be."

"I can imagine," I said.

She sat down on the edge of the bed and wrestled her hair back into what had to be a Kevlar hair tie. Nothing else could've tamed that beast.

I scooted away a tiny bit.

"Speaking of teenage girls," I said, "I found out some stuff about your house." Over the last few days, I'd been to the library and verified most of Grandpa's recollections as correct.

I took a breath, warming to my subject. "The original owner of your house was a family named McFarland. They had a daughter named Stacy. I was able to find out a good bit in archived news articles from the *Vista Point Voice, Wilmington Times,* and *Raleigh News and Record.* There was even a blurb in *USA All Day.*"

Hannah had what looked like a genuine *I hear what you're saying* expression, so I continued. "In June of 1985, the parents went out of town overnight and left Stacy at home alone. She was sixteen. According to the news articles, there was a party toward my end of Bending Oak Drive. Stacy went with Andrew Parker, her next-door neighbor. A guy named Jared Jameson had the party. Stacy's parents came home the next day, and she was gone. They called all the neighbors and her friends. No one had seen Stacy since the party the night before. According to the news articles, Jared Jameson walked her home from the party and was the last person to see her."

Hannah interrupted. "Wait. Why did she *leave* the party with Jared if she *went* with Andrew? Do I smell a love triangle?"

I wrinkled my nose imagining what a love triangle might smell like.

"Maybe Stacy and Andrew had a fight, and that's why Jared walked her home?" Hannah said. "Then when they got home, Jared kissed Stacy goodnight. Since Andrew lived next door, he saw the whole thing, and having secretly loved Stacy for years, he killed Stacy in a fit of jealousy."

"According to the paper, Stacy and Andrew were good friends," I said. "Why would he kill his friend? If he were jealous, wouldn't he go after Jared instead?"

"True." She looked out her bedroom window for a second. "I may have underestimated your emotional intelligence, young Hank."

"Is that a compliment?" I asked.

"Yes," she nodded curtly. "You know, we can't really rely on the news articles. Sometimes the police don't release all the information to the media because they need to keep some facts secret. We need to read the *actual* police report."

"I'm pretty sure they don't make those available to the public."

"Haven't you heard of the Freedom of Information Act?" she asked.

"Yes, but I think that only applies to getting information from the federal government and I don't think it includes kids."

"We'll see. My father's an attorney." She nodded with satisfaction. "I'll talk to him after work tonight."

"I took notes on all the articles I found on microfiche," I said. "They're at my house."

"Okay. If I get my boxes unpacked, maybe we can go back to your house and look at your notes." She stood up and walked toward her closet.

"I'm done out here," I said. "Shove the rest of your clothes in your closet and let's make a run for it."

"Good idea."

As she turned her back, I looked at the yearbook I'd put on her shelf and committed the name, Millview Elementary, to memory.

7

I n 1953, James Watson and Francis Crick discovered the double
helix, the twisted-ladder structure of deoxyribonucleic acid (DNA).
Authorities in Leicestershire, England first used DNA to solve a criminal case in 1987. For more information see Forensics 411 episode 26,
"Double Trouble for Suspects."

ON MY BACK PORCH, I said, "Um, I'll just run and get my notes,
and we can look at them out here."

"Seriously? Can't we go inside? It's so hot," she whined.

"Okay," I answered, not really wanting her to compare my
house to hers.

I led her into the kitchen and watched as she surveyed the
harvest gold appliances and mismatched kitchen chairs that
Mom called "shabby chic." The television was blaring from the
den because Grandpa's mind wasn't the only thing that was
going.

"Grandpa, can you turn that down? Hannah and I have work
to do."

"Go in your bedroom. I can't hear Matlock if I turn the sound
down."

I led Hannah into my room, humbled by my mismatched furniture, forty-year-old carpet, and rumbling window air conditioner. It was the original décor from when the house was new in 1975.

Her eyes got big. "Wow! This is so seventies retro, especially the dark paneling." She looked around. "You really need a lava lamp to finish off the look."

"Thanks," I mumbled. As if any of my decorations, aside from the forensic science and *X-Files* posters, had been personal choices. My room was a compilation of Mom's and Grandpa's love of yard sales and thrift stores.

Hannah sat on the floor of my "vintage" room against my "retro" twin bed to read my handwritten notes. I sat beside her with Chaucer and watched.

She stared at my notes for almost a minute. "Seriously? You're going to watch me read?"

"I guess not." I stood up. "Come on, Chaucer, let's go outside."

He crawled over to where I'd been sitting, put his head in Hannah's lap and sighed.

She looked up. "He can stay. You go." She waved me away with her hand. "I'll text you when I'm done."

Twenty minutes later she did just that. I went back to my room, and she and Chaucer had migrated to my bed.

I sat on the floor.

"Okay," she said, "good note-taking. Let's see if I have everything right. After Jared Jameson's party, around 10:35, Stacy called the Parker's house, asking for Andrew. Andrew didn't go to the phone. The next morning, he called Stacy, but she didn't pick up. He knocked on her front door, but she didn't answer. Later that morning, he left with his family to go on vacation and didn't come back until June fourteenth. By then she'd been gone eight or nine days."

"Yes," I answered. "Stacy's parents came home the day after the party. There were no broken windows or unlocked exterior doors. But when the McFarlands looked closely, they realized some jewelry, candlesticks, and cash were gone."

Hannah continued, "The cops interviewed the neighbors. No one had reported seeing anything suspicious. They searched the house for fingerprints and didn't find any that belonged to anyone other than the McFarland family, Jared, Andrew, and a few of Stacy's friends."

I added, "The articles said after Jared Jameson walked Stacy home from the party, he stayed a few minutes."

"I'd say he stayed more than a *few* minutes if they left the party a little after ten, but he didn't get back home until 10:45." Hannah raised her eyebrows. "It doesn't take forty-five minutes to walk from your end of the street to mine."

"It takes about ten minutes, so that accounts for twenty minutes, round-trip," I said.

"What happened during the other twenty-five minutes?" Hannah asked. "Was he killing her?"

"She was still alive at 10:35 because that's when she called Andrew's house. The phone company verified that."

"They searched for fingerprints, but the articles didn't mention finding any DNA evidence. That's sort of weird."

"She disappeared in 1985. The first U.S. case that cops cracked with DNA evidence wasn't until 1988."

"Oh, I guess that explains why she didn't just text Andrew. It was like the pioneer days back then. Did they even have electricity?"

She shook her head. "And the papers said the Coast Guard searched the waterway and the marsh, right?"

"Yep, and the police had search dogs out looking for her."

Hannah stared at my notebook.

I waited. Had she read to the end of my notes?

Finally, she looked at me with a sparkle in her eyes. "I couldn't help but notice in your notes that you wrote 'COLD CASE NOT RUNAWAY' in all capital letters and underlined it three times with six exclamation points. Am I to take that as a subtle sign that you think the cops messed up, and Stacy didn't rob her own house and run away?"

"Obviously!" I said, taking the notebook from Hannah. "The papers said the cops found a journal in Stacy's locker *two months* after she disappeared, and that it said she was going to run away. Why did it take them two months to search her locker? And did you read what happened to the journal?"

"The cops lost it," Hannah answered.

"According to the articles, Stacy's parents wanted to see the journal. The cops dragged their feet for weeks saying it was evidence and they couldn't let them have it. The McFarlands had to hire a lawyer to see it. When it came time for the cops to show it to them, they couldn't find it. That's a complete violation of the chain of custody. The police reports should document every person who came in contact with a piece of evidence from the crime scene to the courtroom. That alone brings all of the investigation into question!" I shook my head. "Just because there was no sign of a break-in, no unidentified fingerprints, no evidence of foul play, and they never found a body, that doesn't necessarily mean that Stacy robbed her own house and ran away. Someone could've committed the perfect murder. The only proof that Stacy ran away was allegedly in the journal, and it vanished, just like her."

Hannah added, "Her parents said that none of her clothes were missing. Her backpack was still in the kitchen, but the spending money they'd left her was gone. So, we're supposed to believe that she walked out of her house with her hands full of jewelry, candlesticks, and cash, but no clothes? No girl would run away without a change of clothes. And no matter how unhappy she was, wouldn't she eventually get over it and call home?"

"I would think so."

"We need to find that journal," Hannah said. "If we could find it, we could send photos of it to Stacy's mom. She would know if the handwriting was Stacy's or not."

"I looked her up. She's alive and in Raleigh," I said. "You know, if the journal was fake, the whole run-away explanation gets blown to pieces."

Hannah shrugged. "I guess it's stupid to think we could find the journal if the cops couldn't."

"Maybe," I said, "*Unless* they lost it on purpose."

A small smile formed across Hannah's face. "Hmm. Does somebody smell a conspiracy?"

"Yes, and it stinks worse than a love triangle," I answered.

Hannah shook her head. "Dude, you are so weird!"

8

The terms "computer forensics," "digital forensics," and "cyber forensics" are often used interchangeably to describe the application of investigation and analysis techniques to gather and preserve evidence from a computing device in a way that is suitable for presentation in a court of law. See Forensics 411 _episode 25, "Control, Alt, Delete: The Growing Field of Cyber Forensics."_

HANNAH'S DAD confirmed that the Freedom of Information Act didn't apply to kids who wanted to read police investigation files. We needed to get creative.

I went to the back of my closet where I kept a shoe box with the pieces of my stress ball. Over the years, I had whittled away the foam so that now I only carried a small chunk in my pocket. The pieces in the box symbolized my triumph over anxiety. The box also had the journal that Dr. B suggested I keep and my life savings of 247 dollars.

I sat on my bedroom floor and sent a private message to `Hacktivist77` through my _Forensics 411_ page. I'd interviewed him for an episode about computer forensics in seventh grade. It was a fan favorite.

I typed: Have a personal Q. That was how he liked me to inform him that I had a question that might raise red flags with lurkers on my *Forensics 411* page. Hacktivist77 was convinced that the government watched him constantly.

I rubbed Chaucer's ears and scratched his belly while I waited to see if Hacktivist77 would answer me. Chaucer was snoring with his head in my lap when I got a response.

He answered: Can't talk here. What's your phone number?

I considered what my mom had told me a million times about not giving my phone number to anyone online and typed: Can I contact you instead?

I waited.

Two minutes later he private messaged me back: Send your question to the link below. It's encrypted. Will be deleted in five minutes.

I wrote: I need an investigation file from the Vista Point, North Carolina police department. The victim was Stacy McFarland, and the crime happened around June 5, 1985.

He responded: I'll see what I can do.

9

The *Association of Police Communications Officers uses codes to describe situations. A 10-62 means a breaking and entering is in progress, while a 10-68 is the code for livestock in the roadway. For more details see* **Forensics 411** *episode 22, "Talk the Talk."*

HANNAH CAME BY MY HOUSE, her hair still dripping water from swim practice. I filled her in on the latest from `Hacktivist77` as we walked down to the dock with Chaucer.

"I'm impressed that you have a hacker friend to call on," she said as she sat on the dock, kicked off her flip-flops and dipped her feet in the water. We both stared at the water for a minute watching an osprey spruce up its nest. Then my phone pinged, indicating a new message on my *Forensics 411* page.

I clicked on a link. It said: `Digitized records only go back to 2008. Go old school.`

As soon as I finished reading the message it disappeared.

"Cool," Hannah said.

I glanced at her golden hair drying and expanding into snake-like tendrils. "You know, *Medusa*, you might want to get that hair of yours contained before it catches wind and you're lifted away."

She wrinkled her nose. "You're hilarious!" She took a pony-tail holder from around her wrist and went to work on her hair. "So, what do you think he meant by 'going old school'?"

"I think he's suggesting a 10-62."

"10-62?"

"Breaking and entering statute," I explained. "Episode 22."

"Right. More homework for me," she said, finally getting her hair corralled.

"So, he thinks we should break into the police department records room?" she asked.

"I think so."

A devilish smile formed on her face. "That sounds kind of fun. And since we're minors, if they catch us, they'll seal our records and protect our identities. It's the law."

"Oh right, your dad's a lawyer," I answered, not convinced that breaking and entering was the route I wanted to take; nor that if arrested, my mom would be comforted by the sealing of my felony record. "There's got to be some sort of security. I doubt they have filing cabinets full of investigation reports sitting in the lobby for the locals to thumb through."

"I wouldn't be so sure. Dad says the way they do legal stuff around here is really backward, though he didn't phrase it quite so gently."

With the Buckleys in charge of the police department and town hall, her dad was probably right.

I shook my head slowly. "I don't know. We're supposed to be investigating a crime, not committing one."

"Look, if you don't have the chops for it, I'm willing to go it alone."

"That's insubordination."

"It's not insubordination. It's leadership," Hannah declared with a satisfied smile.

"Okay," I said, "I'll do it, but if we get arrested, it was all your idea!"

"Naturally," she said with a big braces-filled smile, "I *am* the brains of this operation."

I nodded. "Just keep telling yourself that."

WE MADE our plans and then used the following afternoon to stake out the police station. First, we stopped at McDiggle's, the fast food restaurant across the street, and got a couple of drinks. Then we propped our bikes against a large moss-draped oak at the end of the police department parking lot and watched, careful to look like we were just hanging out in the shade.

For an hour, we saw a few people enter and exit the front of the building. Around back, there were three portable storage units. About every fifteen minutes, a uniformed officer came out with a set of boxes on a dolly, rolled them into one of the units, then went back into the station for more.

"What do you think's in those boxes?" I asked.

Hannah smiled. "Maybe that's our lobby full of police records."

I scoffed. "Yeah, right."

Hannah looked at my boomerang that I'd set down beside my bike. "Will you teach me how to throw that thing? I figure it must be fun if you take it everywhere."

She'd come a long way from saying it was the official sport of the friendless. "Sure, but we can't do it here. You need a large open space to throw it; otherwise, it can do some damage."

We watched the police station for a few more minutes until Hannah announced, "Okay. I'm ready."

"You sure?"

She nodded. "Let's do this."

I watched Hannah enter the front of the police station. We'd

done our research. If all went well, she would go in and introduce herself to Marcia Masters, the sixty-something lady who
worked the front desk from eight to five, five days a week. On
the weekends it was Joanne Lubbock. We liked our chances
better with Marcia because she seemed to be a bit of a gossip on
Facebook. Hannah could get her talking.

She would tell Marcia that she was writing a story for a
contest and needed to learn about police investigation reports,
what they looked like, and how to write and organize one. If all
went well, Officer Masters would give her the grand tour of the
records room.

Thirty minutes later Hannah came back outside.

"Well?" I asked.

"No tour, but I got Marcia Masters talking. They are in the
process of clearing and renovating the records room. `Hack-
tivist77` was right. They have digitized all records from the
present back to 2008. They are currently moving the files from
before 2008 to the portable storage units behind the station. Then
they're going to move them off-site to permanent storage."

We moved our bikes behind the center storage unit and
watched the same officer rolling boxes.

The officer's phone rang. "Hang on honey, you're breaking
up." He moved closer to the building. "Okay, now I can hear
you."

"Merry Christmas to us!" Hannah whispered, grabbing my
hand to lead me around the side of the trailer.

We listened to his side of the conversation. "What? Your
water broke? The baby's coming?"

Hannah moved with the precision of a pick-pocket and took
the keys from the padlock of the trailer.

"Yeah, just let me tell Marcia, and I'll be home in ten minutes.
Don't you have that baby without me!" He listened. "I love you
too. I'll be there soon."

While we dashed around to the back of the storage units, the
officer rolled the dolly with boxes on it into the unit, pulled the

door down and reached for the lock. He looked on the ground around him. We watched him pat down his pockets, shrug, then go inside.

In a few minutes, Marcia Masters came out and locked the storage unit with her own key.

10

Detailed records must document every person who handles evidence from crime scene to courtroom. Each is a link in the chain of custody. See Forensics 411 _episode 5, "The Chain of Custody."_

THAT NIGHT WAS the first time I ever crawled out my bedroom window. It was the most disobedient thing I'd ever done. Not that I was really _disobeying_ my mom—I hadn't asked if I could go out at 11:30 to steal a file from the Vista Point police. It was more like failing to tell her about my felonious plans.

Hannah and I met at the big oak tree across from her house. We rode our bikes two miles to the police station, stashed them in the woods behind the building and waited. It was almost midnight.

There was no activity at the back of the station, and McDiggle's, across the street, closed at eleven. As the last Mc-workers drifted to their cars, we headed full-on into our first 10-64, which was a crime in progress. Technically, since we had keys to the storage unit, we weren't committing a 10-62.

We donned ski masks that belonged to Hannah and wore

57

latex gloves as we tried the keys on the first storage trailer until we found one that worked. The dolly was still at the front of the unit, loaded with boxes. We rolled the door most of the way down, giving ourselves a couple of inches for air. I took off my mask, reached in the side pocket of my backpack for my flashlight.

Hannah took off her mask and whispered, "Marcia Masters told me the files are grouped by the year the crime was reported and investigated. If a file has a separate box of evidence that goes with it, there will be an orange sticker on the front of the folder."

I aimed my light at the boxes on the dolly. They were all labeled 2006.

We shone our lights on boxes in the back of the storage trailer. Hannah whispered, "Those boxes back there are all from the 2000s. I guess that means the 1985 files are in a different storage unit."

We put our masks back on, locked the first trailer and moved to the next one.

"Let's hope it's one that's still here and hasn't already been moved to permanent storage."

We tried the same key on the center storage unit, but it didn't work. One by one we tried the other keys from the collection on the key ring. They were all the same color, size, and basic shape so we figured they must all go to the padlocks on the storage units.

The fifth key we tried worked. We rolled the door up about two feet and crawled under. I pushed it most of the way back down, turned on my flashlight and we removed our masks. We could hardly move around the tightly packed boxes.

I shined my light on a box at the front.

"1988," Hannah said. "Give me a boost. I think I can fit across the top of the boxes to see what's in the next row."

I laced my fingers together to make a place for her foot.

"Okay, lift," she said.

I gave her a boost, and she smacked the top of her head on the ceiling.

"Jeez," she said rubbing her head. "You don't have to throw me across the trailer!"

"My bad."

I tried again successfully, and she inched her way across the top of the boxes with her flashlight.

"Just be quick. It's getting hot in here." I used my mask to wipe my face.

Hannah slithered around peeking at boxes. "I've got some files from 1985," she said. "They're supposed to be in alphabetical order." Her voice faded as she moved farther toward the back of the unit. "Pull some of those boxes at the front off the stacks, so I have room to move things around."

I did as ordered, and heard more boxes open and close. My watch said 12:49. "Hurry up."

She said, "Got it!" and her feet appeared above my head.

"Okay, I'm coming down. Don't let me fall."

Her shins appeared, then her knees. "Um… where am I supposed to… grab you," I asked.

"Around the hips," she answered, as if that should've been obvious.

Nothing about touching a girl was obvious to me.

I directed her legs down the front of the stacked boxes and accidentally felt a hip bone as I lowered her to the floor.

"Good job," she said.

"Thanks," I answered, glad we were in the dark and she couldn't see my red face.

We put our ski masks back on and eased under the door. I locked it, and we crept off to the woods where we'd left our bikes.

Hannah looked at the McFarland file. "There's no orange sticker," she said, "so there's no separate evidence box. That means Stacy's journal was in this folder at some point. How did the journal disappear, but the file's still here?"

She handed over the folder, which was about an inch thick and smelled like a wet dog. I tucked it into my backpack.

"Do you want to go through it tonight?" I asked.

Hannah looked at her watch. "It's late. I don't think I should push my luck. If my parents figure out that I'm not in my room, there will be lectures, surveillance, and Mama-drama."

"I know how that is." Nothing freaked out my mom more than when I disappeared. "I'll bring the file down to your house in the morning, and we'll read it there."

"Right," she whispered, "like you're not going to go home and read that file from cover to cover!"

I put my right hand in the air. "I solemnly swear that I will not read the file without you," I said, getting on my bike to pedal.

Very sincerely, she said, "You should know, I don't tolerate disloyalty."

11

L ocard's Exchange Principle states that every contact a person or
animal makes with another person, place, or object results in an
exchange of physical materials. See Forensics 411 episode 2, "Rate of
Exchange."

HANNAH TEXTED ME AT 7:45. R U coming or what?

I typed: do ur parents care if I show up this
early?

She responded: Come thru backyard & into
basement.

SHE MET me in her driveway and led me to the bottom floor
which she called their "in-law suite." We sat at a small table, so
close I could smell her fruity shampoo.

I placed both hands on the table, ready to read my first
genuine police investigation file. I would be like a real investigator, reading the interview transcripts and analyzing the evidence
list. It would be an in-depth look into what the investigators

found, what they were thinking at the time, and how they concluded that Stacy robbed her own house and ran away.

Except it wasn't.

Hannah opened the folder. "Let's start from the beginning at the same time."

The first few pages recapped the basics that we already knew from the news articles, but a detailed list of missing items on page seven caught our eye.

I scoffed. "They must have had a lot of money—look at the list of jewelry. Do you have your tablet around? I'd like to see what 'a men's gold nugget bracelet' and 'women's diamond tennis bracelet' look like."

"It's upstairs in my room."

While Hannah was gone, I snooped around the living-dining area. I cracked open a closed door and peeked into what looked like a shrine to the Pittsburgh Steelers. Football posters covered the walls. The twin beds had matching Steelers bedspreads. "*That's* why she's `GirlofSteel`," I mumbled to myself. Small trophies and photos lined the bookshelves. I moved to take a closer look, but heard footsteps coming down the stairs and shot back to the table.

Hannah came back in, glanced to the left, and made a seamless move to close the door to the Steelers bedroom. I took a deep breath and flipped a page of the report while she powered up her tablet.

"Wow, Mr. McFarland must've been a flashy guy, this thing is hideous."

She showed me the gold nugget bracelet photo.

"Gross," I said.

Hannah nodded. "Let's see what a tennis bracelet looks like." She turned the tablet back. "Ooh, now that's pretty. Lots of diamonds."

I thumbed through the remaining pages of the investigation report. "Have you noticed there are no transcripts from the interviews they conducted? Interview transcripts should be in the file unless there's a notation somewhere in the report that they're stored separately. Did you see anything?"

"Nope," she answered.

I flipped through the folder. "There's also not a map of the search area. The news stories said that they had search dogs out looking for Stacy. There should be a map with the search area marked. There should be details about which law enforcement agency the dogs worked for." The lack of professionalism shown by the Vista Point police irritated me.

"Oh wait," Hannah interjected, "I just read something about that." She took the pages off the table and shuffled through them. "Here it is." She read the sheet and laughed. "It says 'all surrounding areas were searched.' I guess they didn't need a map because they searched everywhere."

"All 197 million square miles of Earth?" I grunted. "Clearly the investigator who wrote this report had no idea what he was doing. It's no wonder he lost Stacy's journal." I flipped the file to the very last page to find the name of the officer who signed the report. "Holy crap!"

"What?" Hannah asked.

"The investigation was headed by Bob Buckley!"

"Who's that?"

"He's the mayor of Vista Point. He and my grandpa have hated each other since high school." I shook my head. "Mayor Buckley liked my grandmother, but Grandpa won her over. I never knew he was a cop. When the news articles about Stacy's disappearance referred to 'Officer Buckley,' I assumed they were talking about Chester Buckley, the current police chief. They're brothers."

Hannah said, "If Bob Buckley didn't do a bang-up job writing the report, maybe he didn't do a good job looking for Stacy either? There could be people he didn't interview or places he didn't search. Even if he did say he searched *everywhere*." She added, "Are the mayor and police chief related to Dillon Buckley?"

An imaginary atomic bomb exploded in my head. "Why do you ask?"

"Some girls on the swim team pointed him out to me."

"Were they making fun of him?" (I wished! The girls thought Dillon was a "hottie.")

"Well... I don't think so," Hannah answered. "What? Do people not like him? I kind of got the impression he was popular."

"Not exactly," I answered, thinking I could promulgate the biggest hoax since the Jackalope if I could convince Hannah that the masses despised Dillon Buckley. "He walks around like he's head boy of some British boarding school."

"The Draco Malfoy of Vista Point?" Hannah said with a British accent.

"Pretty much."

Hannah sat back in her chair and looked out the window. After a long silence, she clasped her hands on the table.

"The other day, I overheard some girls on the swim team talking. They were calling you 'Boomer' and I set them straight on that."

I tried not to groan. "Thanks." I'm sure they had a field day with that. "What did they say?"

"There's this girl on the team named Lexi."

I narrowed my eyes. "Lexi Nguyen? The girl who walks around looking like she's trying to divide five-hundred-thirteen by twenty-three but just ran out of fingers?"

Hannah burst out laughing and pounded the table with her hand. "Oh, my gosh, yes! That captures her essence perfectly. She's the walking confused."

I couldn't believe that air-headed Lexi Nguyen was going to divulge the secret of my low approval rating. I swallowed hard. "And?" I asked, waiting for the bomb to drop.

"She and some other girls were laughing about some question that `AutopsyAl` asked on *Forensics 411*."

I exhaled my relief. They all made fun of my show, but that didn't bother me. How could such limited people understand?

"Yeah, `AutopsyAl` has been following me since sixth grade, when I started *Forensics 411*. He asks questions like: 'If I pee sitting down, does that make me transgender?'" I rolled my eyes. "He's pretty clueless, but a loyal follower."

"Are you sure?" she asked.

"Yeah, I feel sorry for him. I think I might be the only friend he has. But sometimes it takes me hours to answer his questions in a way I think he'll understand."

"That's sweet," Hannah said, putting her hand on my arm. I didn't even flinch.

"So, were Lexi and her posse making fun of `AutopsyAl`? That wouldn't surprise me. They're vicious to a girl at school with Down's Syndrome."

"That's awful," she answered. "No, they were laughing because they said that `AutopsyAl` is really Dillon Buckley and that he asks those stupid questions to yank your chain."

My face got hot, and I could think of nothing to say. All the years of my life I'd wasted trying to be nice to `AutopsyAl`, and it was all a lie.

"He sounds like a jerk!" Hannah said. "I just wanted to tell you because I read the questions he asked, and I read your well-thought-out answers. And... well..." She took her hand off my arm and shrugged her shoulders. "I just wanted you to know the truth. Like I said, loyalty is important to me."

"Um... thanks," I answered, warmed by her allegiance to me, but furious at Dillon for making a fool of me, and at myself for falling for it.

"Did you hear anything else about Dillon and me?" I asked.

"No, why?"

She'd find out soon enough. "We don't get along. In first grade, I accidentally knocked him out cold on the playground with my boomerang. He told the principal I did it on purpose and that I'd been picking on him since kindergarten, which I hadn't. When he passed out, he peed in his pants, and for weeks the kids sang, 'Dillon-needs-a-diaper. Dillon-needs-a-diaper.' His older cousin Rodney, who was in high school at the time, trolled the playground ready to hurt anyone who dared mention the contents of Dillon's pants. He actually hit a kid!"

"Sounds like a great family," Hannah said.

"You may see Rodney from time to time around town picking up roadkill."

"Roadkill?" Hannah asked. "Does he work for Animal Control?"

"No," I answered. "He eats animals that have been hit by cars! Rodney lives in a school bus out in the middle of nowhere and belongs to some survivalist group that considers possum a tasty treat."

Hannah scoffed. "You're kidding—right?"

"Nope. Vista Point is full of some weird people, and Rodney is the weirdest. He keeps an electric slow cooker in his trunk so he can whip up a stew anytime. There was an article in the *Vista Point Voice* a few years ago."

Hannah gagged. "We should probably stick together when school starts."

I wanted to jump up and down in agreement. But instead, I very smoothly said, "Yeah, let's do that."

Raising an imaginary glass, Hannah said, "May Dillon Buckley forever walk around with his zipper down and a piece of toilet paper stuck to the bottom of his shoe!"

"Here, here," I answered, raising my own invisible glass.

She looked around the room and added, "So, should we get back to work on the file?"

"Sure," I answered, knowing that my Dillon problem wouldn't go away, but feeling excited that for once, I might have another person on Team Boomer. I mean *Team Hank*.

(I was still struggling with my new persona.)

As we read the report, we learned a few things that hadn't been in the news articles. Mr. McFarland had left his brand-new convertible in the driveway. Every exterior door of their house had a deadbolt lock. You needed a key to lock or unlock them, even from the inside. Also, Stacy's house keys were sitting on the kitchen counter when her parents got home. When the McFarlands went through the house with the police, they noted that a lawn chair laying on the floor of the garage usually hung on the wall. Finally, the report said they never recovered any of the stolen goods.

I was completing my notes when Hannah finished her second read-through. She burst out laughing.

"What?" I asked.

"Did you see the picture of Stacy's journal?" She held up a Polaroid photo.

"Yep," I answered. It didn't seem like anything funny to me.

She shoved it closer to me. "Look at this. It's ridiculous!"

The picture showed a green spiral notebook with the words "Stacy's Journal" written on the center of the cover in black marker surrounded by a random collection of hastily scribbled rebellious phrases like "THE WORLD SUCKS."

"Yeah, they should've taken pictures of every single page. That way, they'd have had it to show Stacy's parents even after they lost the journal."

She rolled her eyes. "You're such a boy!"

She set the photo of the journal cover on the table. "No girl would *ever* keep a journal in a spiral notebook with the words 'Stacy's Journal' written on the cover—unless she were like—seven! And she sure wouldn't scrawl 'I like boys' on it. That's so lame. A spiral notebook—please!"

Hannah stared at the photo of Stacy's journal for a moment. "That's it! That's what's wrong with all of this!" She pointed to my notebook full of McFarland case research.

I looked at her. "What?"

"First of all, any girl who keeps a journal is going to be very protective of it, so why would she have taken it to school with her? The news reports said the cops found the journal in her school locker, right?"

"Yeah," I answered. "Maybe she took the journal with her to school every day so that her parents wouldn't read it? I mean, if she did have a drug problem and were planning to run away, she wouldn't want her parents to know that."

"But if you're trying to keep your misery and drug problem a secret, why would you write that 'drugs are cool' on the outside of your journal? Girls just don't write stuff like that. They draw flowers and stars and doodles—maybe hearts. Trust me!"

"Plus, there's the whole issue of the journal being in her locker *all summer*," Hannah added. "You and I went to different schools, but I think they all do the same thing with lockers at the end of the school year."

"What?" I kept all my stuff in my book bag, preferring to risk scoliosis than to subject myself to the pitfalls that came with locker ownership.

She smacked her lips. "Think about it! During the last couple of days of school, the teachers always make you take everything out of your locker. Then you have to leave the locker standing wide open so the teachers can inspect it. They have to be sure they get all their textbooks and calculators back."

"Oh yeah," I answered, embarrassed that I hadn't thought of that myself.

"I don't see how she could have 'accidentally' left her journal in her locker for the whole summer without someone noticing. Teachers are down-right militant about making sure students thoroughly clean out their lockers."

I opened my notebook to the pages where I had taken notes on each of the news articles. "You're right!" I pointed. "The earliest news article that mentions the journal was dated August 20, 1985. It said that investigators found the notebook in Stacy's locker at Vista Point High the day before."

"So, we're supposed to believe that she left her journal in her locker on June fifth and *no one* noticed it until August nine-teenth?" Hannah asked. "Not a teacher or a custodian? No one?"

"And why would the police not check her locker before August nineteenth?" I asked. "She disappeared on the *last* day of school!"

I looked down at one of the pages of the report. "Bob Buckley signed this report on August 18, 1985. But the newspapers said the cops found the journal on August 19th."

"Maybe he got his dates mixed up," Hannah suggested.

"That's possible, but I'm even more convinced that Stacy didn't run away."

"Why?" Hannah asked.

"It's too perfect," I explained. "A house gets robbed. A girl disappears. You can't find a body. There's no sign of forced entry. After months of no leads, he finds a journal that 'proves' that Stacy ran away. Then *that* disappears too! It's so perfect it's impossible."

Hannah looked at me. "Should these reports and notes be originals?"

"What do you mean?" I looked over at the file.

She pointed to the top left corner of one page, and then another. "This is a copy. See the imprint of the staple here?"

I thumbed through the pages. "You're right. They're all copies."

"Is that important?"

"Very."

"Why?" she asked.

"Exactly," I answered.

Hannah grunted. "I hate when you answer my *why* questions with *exactly!*"

"*Why* isn't the original report here? Where could it be? There's no reason for photocopies of the actual report. Reports should only have copies or photos of evidence that's in a secondary evidence box."

She peered out the window. "I think the answer is right here."

"In your basement?" I asked.

"No, Boy Genius, here on our property. My gut tells me the answer is out there." She pointed to her back yard. "We need to do our *own* search of the area."

"Good idea. My grandfather has a metal detector. I'll go get it, and we can search your yard."

"I'll put the file back in order. Do you want me to keep it here?"

"I think we should return it tonight just in case someone goes looking for it," I said. "You game?"

"I better not. Sneaking out two nights in a row might be asking for trouble. But I do think we should take pictures of the entire file. I'll do that with my tablet while you get the metal detector. Okay?"

"Good idea."

Hannah reassembled the folder and started taking photos of each page as I left.

12

A *ny decent metal detector can find most metal objects, even those made of gold, silver, brass, and bronze. For more information on metal detectors, watch* Forensics 411 *episode 11, "Can You Dig It?"*

WHEN I CAME BACK with the metal detector, Hannah was waiting in her driveway.

"Do you think we'll find some pirate treasure?"

"Grandpa got this at a pawn shop. He took up treasure-hunting as a hobby after my grandma died. It's a good one—can detect all the precious metals. Moist soil increases electromagnetic conductivity, which helps the mechanism detect deeply buried metals. The sandy soil is well-drained, so it doesn't hold moisture for long. But the black loamy soil retains—"

Hannah put her hand in the air. "Stop. It was a rhetorical question. No need to go all Hankapedia on me."

I lowered my head, embarrassed that I didn't know when to shut up. It was an ongoing problem.

"It's okay. Sometimes you're just a bit too knowledgeable."

That's what Mom called being a know-it-all.

"No one's perfect, and sometimes your disquisitions are

useful," she said, "like when you explained why you shouldn't let your dog drink salt water. Someday, that could come in handy."

We took turns swinging the metal detector from side to side while we searched every inch of her yard, front and back, and didn't find anything but screws and rusty nails.

As we moved into the woods south of Hannah's house, she offered me a piece of gum.

"Are you allowed to have that with braces?" I asked.

"What are you, the dental police?"

"No, just concerned about your parent's financial investment in your mouth. You're only allowed to break a bracket so many times before Dr. Marchini fires you for non-compliance."

She giggled. "Jeez, getting fired by your orthodontist is the ultimate rejection." Then she squinted at me and said, "How'd you know he's my orthodontist?"

"He's the only one in Vista Point."

She countered, "I could go to one in Wilmington."

"True, but I assumed that your parents would be convenience-oriented. Most adults are."

She stopped walking and said, "Do you want a piece of gum or not?"

"What flavor?"

"Blue raspberry."

"No thanks. I don't eat blue food."

"You don't actually *eat* gum, you *chew* it. And when all the genetically-engineered flavor is gone, you throw it away."

"I don't *chew* blue food, either," I answered.

She shrugged. "Suit yourself."

We covered an acre or so, but still found nothing that seemed relevant.

"Let's quit for today and head to the library," I suggested.

"What's there?"

"Books and air conditioning."

Hannah smiled. "Two of my favorite things!"

"WHAT ARE WE RESEARCHING?" she whispered, as we entered the library.

"Stacy's journal." I led her through the aisles of books to the local history section.

"Do we have reason to believe that Stacy's journal is available for check-out?"

I stopped in front of a shelf near the back window. "No. We're looking for this." I pointed to a Vista Point High School yearbook from 1985. "I'd like to see what Stacy looked like, so I can picture her in my mind. And," I said as I turned the pages, "we're looking for the name of the school custodian. Maybe we can track him down."

"Well, let's hope he was young back then; otherwise he might be dead by now."

Hannah flipped to the index to find Stacy's name. "Wow. She's on a lot of pages. And she's pretty," she said, as we found her class picture. She had long brown hair with bangs that stood two inches above the rest of her head. "Now that's some eighties hair!" Hannah chuckled.

We continued turning pages. "And look—she was the captain of the JV cheerleaders. And here she is again, the class secretary."

Hannah pointed to her photo with the rest of the class officers. "Look at that smile. She doesn't look miserable or addicted to drugs." Then she motioned to a boy standing next to Stacy in the photo. "That's Andrew Parker, her next-door neighbor. It says he was the class treasurer."

"Let's go to the faculty and staff pictures," I said.

"They were toward the back." Hannah flipped pages. "Here."

I leaned over her shoulder to get a better look. "Okay, custodian's name was... holy crap."

Hannah looked to where my finger was pointing and read aloud. "Calvin Taylor." She giggled. "Check out his box cut. He looks young there. He's probably still alive. Let's check the most recent Vista Point High yearbook and see if he still works there."

"He doesn't," I told her.

"How do you know?" Hannah asked.

"Because he's Chaucer's veterinarian."

"Wow—janitor to doctor—that's upward mobility!"

13

A *person with antisocial personality disorder can be prone to fighting and has little regard for the safety of others. See* **Forensics 411** *episode 42, "Dangerous Minds," for an overview of mental health issues related to crime.*

THAT NIGHT I answered a few questions about poisoning from my *Forensics 411* followers then set out for the station, this time alone. I climbed out my bedroom window at 11:30 p.m. with the *Mission Impossible* song playing in my head.

I tiptoed across the deck outside my window and into the backyard. *Crime Cat* knocked gently against the dock as I pictured Hannah sitting there on the weathered planks with her feet dangling in the water, her crazy-curly hair in full-scale rebellion, chewing blue gum.

With the McFarland file tucked in my backpack, I wheeled my bike away from the house. Staying under the boughs of the gnarled oaks that lined our neighborhood streets, I pedaled along back roads while heat lightning intermittently illuminated the night sky. When I got to the station, I propped my bike against the back of the middle storage trailer, put on my mask, latex gloves, and got to work.

I was reaching for the padlock keys in my pocket when someone came up behind me, ripped off my mask, and said, "Stop right there!"

I froze.

An arm wrapped around my shoulder from behind and pulled me to the ground. Suddenly the masked attacker was on top of me, his knees pinning my arms to my sides. "Don't even think about moving," the voice commanded.

I couldn't respond. With a grunt, I squirmed beneath his weight, trying to get free. But something was wrong—more wrong than the fact that I had a person sitting on top of me in a dark parking lot at midnight. My assailant didn't weigh much more than I did. I inhaled, and my nose knew. That cologne he bathed in clung to him.

"Buckley! Get off me!" I flailed around, trying to get my arms out from under his legs, but Dillon was stronger than me.

"Don't bother to fight, Forensic Freak!" he grunted.

That only made me more determined. There was no way I would get beat by him again. He'd issued many invitations for me to throw down over the years, but I did my best not to accommodate him. Mom always looked so sad when I came home beat up. But that night, in the empty parking lot, I fought back. There were no bystanders to rate my battle skills on some random online survey generated by people who should have been doing homework or mandatory community service. No one was videoing it for Instagram. For once, it was a fair fight with no witnesses.

Witnesses were the worst, especially when they cheered against you.

Anger boiled inside me as I tried to use the strength of my legs to flip him off my body.

He laughed. "God, you're such a wuss! I bet the new girl could kick your ass."

I thrust my legs upward and threw him off me. Then I jerked my head up and nailed him in the chin with it.

While he grabbed his jaw, I stumbled backward and straightened up.

He dove at me, wrapping his hands around my waist and sending me to the gravel.

"I've been checking out your new friend at the pool." He grunted. "She's got a nice rack, but seriously, how's a white girl grow an Afro?"

I scrambled to a standing position when he crossed the line of civilized engagement by kneeing me in the groin. I gasped and crumbled back to the ground.

He glowered above me. "Last night, I was hanging at The Compound having a couple of brewskies with my bro and his friends when I saw you two sneaking around. Surely you two aren't..." He shook his head, "Nah, there's no way that girl would let you... unless she's mental." He raised his eyebrow. "That would make sense."

"You're... the one that's mental, `AutopsyAl`!" I said between gasps.

He cackled. "Congratulations! You just figured out Blue's Clues. It only took you three years! You really are a super genius!" Dillon put his hand up to his mouth. "Guess I'm busted." He wiped sweat from his face. "But then I'm not the one trying to break into the police trailers." He shook his head. "I have to tell you, Crime Kid, this doesn't look good. Doesn't look good at all!"

I tried to stand, but the throbbing pain, radiating in every direction, paralyzed me.

"Of course, I'll have to tell Uncle Chester what I saw here tonight. He'll need to investigate."

He flipped me over and tore the book bag off my back.

"No!" I yelled, fighting the urge to vomit.

He ripped it open and reached inside, coming out with the

McFarland file. His lip curled in disgust. "What? You do homework in the summer? What a loser!"

He held the folder like a frisbee and threw it across the parking lot. The contents flew in every direction.

I climbed to all fours to grab my backpack, relieved by Dillon's stupidity.

"Tell ya what," he said. "I won't tell Uncle Chester. We'll call it even with this—" and he punched me squarely in the face.

Blood exploded from my nose.

I heard him yell, "See ya, Freak!" just before I vomited.

After Dillon disappeared, I wiped blood from my face and scanned the parking lot. It wasn't windy, but the papers had flown all over the place.

Unable to stand because of the pain, I crawled around the parking lot and the woods behind the station, picking up the contents of the McFarland file sheet by sheet, trying to not drip blood on them. When I didn't see any more papers, I pulled myself to a crouching position and rolled my bike over to a large tree at the back of the parking lot. I reassembled the file as I sat against the tree, waiting for the nausea and throbbing to go away.

An hour later, maybe six, I could finally stand. I looked at the trailers and knew I didn't have the energy to climb over the wall of boxes to return the McFarland file to the right place. Instead, I wiped my fingerprints off the padlock keys and tossed them toward the trailers. Someone from the station would find them. Slowly, I limped my bike home with the McFarland file tucked back in my bookbag.

I was more determined than ever to solve the McFarland mystery with Hannah. We'd become famous and inseparable—like Batman and Robin, except Robin left Batman to become Nightwing. That wouldn't happen with us. After solving the case, we'd be actual celebrities, together. I'd make an episode of *Forensics 411* that would explode. I'd hit a thousand followers, and Hannah would be at my side.

Biting down on my lip, I climbed back through my bedroom window. It was 2:57 in the morning. I stowed the McFarland file in my closet, then shuffled to the bathroom.

In the mirror, dried blood streaked my face and swollen nose.

I took a deep breath, washed my face, brushed my teeth, and moved to the freezer for ice.

Mom's door squeaked open. "Boomer? Is that you?"

I didn't turn around. "Yeah, I'm just getting a drink."

"Okay. Sleep tight. Love you."

"Love you, too," I answered back as I shoved ice into a plastic baggie and wrapped it in a towel. I held it over my nose until, eventually, I drifted off to sleep.

14

B ruises, *also called contusions, result from damage to small blood vessels at the site of blunt-force trauma. See* Forensics 411 *episode 8, "The Truth in Black and Blue" for more details.*

THE FOLLOWING DAY I slept late enough that Mom didn't see me before she went to work.

It was one of the days she dragged Grandpa to the senior citizen center. He hated it, but Mom didn't give him a choice. He'd say things like, "You're not the boss of me!" Even as the words spilled from his mouth, I could see in his eyes that he was lying, and he knew it. As Grandpa's dementia worsened, their parent-child relationship slowly reversed, and Mom was the one making decisions. I hated to watch his authority and dignity disappear with his memory.

I surveyed the damage to my face in my bedroom mirror. My long nose was still swollen, so I grabbed more ice and sat down at the computer to unleash some revenge on Dillon.

I typed the name of the neighborhood pool into the search engine. The pool manager's name was Deborah Jenkins. I logged into one of the anonymous email accounts that I used for covert ops and typed a message to her.

```
Ms. Jenkins,

We are members of the pool. My daughter
swims there almost every day. She came
home yesterday and told me that a boy
named Dillon Buckley has been sneaking
into the girl's locker room and watching
the girls change clothes.

She doesn't want me to share her name
because she is afraid that the boy will
find out that she's the one that told.

Can you please make sure this boy stays
out of the girl's locker room?

Sincerely,
    A Concerned Parent
```

I hit "send" and chuckled to myself. "That should get you banned from the pool for a couple of weeks, and keep you away from Hannah!"

I GOT to Hannah's around eleven in the morning with my swelling under control, but not gone.

"What happened to your face?" she asked as she opened her front door.

"Born this way," I mumbled.

"No, I mean your nose. It's swollen."

"I ran into the storage unit at the police station last night."

"Did you take the file back?"

"Yes." I looked up at the sky. "We better get started before it gets too hot."

We moved into the part of the woods beside her house that we hadn't searched the day before and got to work.

From behind Hannah asked, "Are you limping?"

"Yes, fine. I'm limping!" I snapped. "I tripped in the parking lot when I was taking the file back."

She covered her mouth to stifle a giggle. "Looks like you had a rough night. Here," she reached out and took the metal detector from my hands, "I'll do that."

After an eternity, we heard the beep of the metal detector. "Probably just another nail," Hannah said. "We've got enough to build a house."

With latex gloves on, I bent down and cleared away decaying leaves and pine needles while Hannah held the detector over the area. I winced. Hunching over reminded me of my slide across the gravel parking lot the night before.

As I removed leaves, the beeps got louder.

Hannah said, "You're getting closer!"

I dug deeper with my hands. Finally, "I've got something!"

"Let me see. What is it?"

As I tugged harder on the object, the resistance lessened. "It's not a nail. It feels like a chain!"

I held the object up to the light that filtered between the trees. I shook away the fine black soil that was native to the coast, then wiped it clean with my gloved hand.

Hannah pointed. "Oh my god! That's a gold nugget bracelet!"

I looked at the inside. We knew from the police report that Michael McFarland's initials were engraved on the underside of the bracelet. "I can't tell if there are initials or not. Let's take it to the water."

Twenty yards away, the Intracoastal Waterway ran behind our entire neighborhood. Hannah set the metal detector down, and I dipped the gold bracelet into the water to remove the remaining dirt.

I rinsed and held it so we could see if there was any engraving. "That's it!" Hannah cried out. "Those are his initials."

"It's official! We just got our first break!"

"Do you think the robber was in these woods and dropped it?" she asked.

"If the robber were in these woods, what was he doing here?" I turned a circle looking around the wooded area. "Maybe Stacy's buried here." As always, I yearned for the ground-penetrating radar that cops used to find bodies.

"Well, we know one thing for sure," Hannah said, "if this bracelet has been right here, next to where the McFarlands lived, the cops didn't search 'everywhere' very well. They probably missed all kinds of clues. Should we take this to the cops?" Hannah asked.

"Are you kidding? We can't trust the cops! We've got to do this on our own."

15

A contusion goes through color-changes as the body heals. The color of a bruise typically goes from dark blue to a lighter blue to a greenish-yellow, to just yellow, then fades after about two weeks.See Forensics 411 *episode 8, "The Truth in Black and Blue."*

I DODGED my mom and grandpa that night and the next day, so they didn't see my bruised face. Mom works a lot, and sometimes Grandpa is so engrossed in what he's watching on television that he forgets I'm around.

Hannah and I took a break from the case to visit Pelican Island just across the waterway from our neighborhood. It was Chaucer's favorite place to let his nose go crazy. No one lived on the island, and most of it was a protected nature preserve, only reachable by boat. I loved it, and so did Chaucer.

A storm had blown through the night before, so it would be cool to check out the damage to the island.

"Maybe the wash-over unearthed some pirate treasure," I suggested, trying to get Hannah as enthusiastic about our day on the island as Chaucer was.

We beached *Crime Cat* at Oyster Cove on the north end of the island, and seemed to have the island to ourselves. After setting the anchor, I unloaded the boat and Hannah set up the beach umbrella to give us some shade. Chaucer whined, begging me to let him go chase birds.

"Come get some water first, then you can go play." He bounced over to me when he saw his bowl, quickly lapped the water into his mouth, then looked at me expectantly, wagging his tail.

"Okay, you can go." He let out a howl then took off in a full run toward a flock of sandpipers. I loved to see him that happy, getting to be a hound dog.

"Will he come back on his own? What if he goes in the water? Can he swim?"

"He won't go too far, and he'll come back on his own. He always does. And he's a bloodhound; it's not like they get lost easily. Besides, I want to show you the island. We'll catch up to him."

I slid the water bowl into the shade of the umbrella as Hannah removed her shorts and t-shirt to reveal a tiny, two-piece bathing suit. *Had she grabbed Josey's by mistake?*

I swallowed hard. My eyes, with a mind of their own, gawked at her. I'd never seen her in a bathing suit other than the ugly one-piece, navy-blue swim team suit, which bound and gagged the parts that this smaller, less-comprehensive suit did not.

Her skin was tan and contrasted with her hair that had lightened up a lot over the summer.

I wiped sweat from my lip. What Dillon said was true. Feeling embarrassed, I spun toward the umbrella.

"Did you know that the serving size of a pickle is three-fourths of a pickle?"

"What?" she asked.

"The serving size of a pickle—it's only seventy-five percent of the pickle. Mathematically, it doesn't seem right, because pickles come in a variety of sizes. Three-fourths of one pickle could be 100 percent of a smaller pickle." I rattled on. "I think they really need to come up with a uniform pickle size. I mean, where do gherkins fall on the pickle spectrum?" I couldn't face her.

"This is scandalous. Have you contacted the major pickle manufacturers?"

"I've sent out a few emails but haven't heard anything back yet," I answered while staring at my troll feet.

"Well, don't let them off the hook," she said with conviction. "Someone needs to be held accountable." Then she continued, "Not to steer the subject away from the all-mighty pickle, but I brought some books. Have you read any of these?" I watched her shadow hold up several books like the models on *The Price Is Right*.

"Um... no," I responded, stealing a quick look without turning around.

"Do you want to read one? I brought plenty, so pick which one you want."

I watched her shadow on the ground coming closer to mine. Soon it was right beside me. I wanted so badly to turn around and look at her in 3-D, but I just couldn't.

"So, what'll it be? Do you want to read one of these?"

I turned my torso, holding my left hand out while averting my eyes from her nearly-naked body. "I'll take that one," I answered, as I grabbed the book from her hand and spun back around.

"Really?" she said with a giggle. "You do surprise me sometimes."

I read the title and groaned. Sure, I wanted to read a book about a love triangle between a girl, a vampire, and a pterodactyl. Didn't every guy?

"You want some water?"

"Sure," I answered as I sat down in a chair under the umbrella and pretended to delve into the stupid book.

Much later, Hannah laughed. "You might enjoy the book more if it were right-side up."

I looked down, embarrassed to see the upside-down book, as if choosing the stupid pre-historic, paranormal romance wasn't bad enough.

"I'm actually trying to train myself to read upside down," I said in defense of my idiocy.

"Is that a lost art, like boomeranging?" she teased.

"That's right! It *is* a lost art," I answered feeling angry at her for wearing a bikini that made me want to look at her like I wanted to look at her.

She pulled her phone out of the beach bag. "Shouldn't we go look for Chaucer? He's been gone a while."

I sat up. He had completely slipped my mind as I simmered in a hot skillet of hormones. "Yeah, we need to catch up with him."

"I'll grab some waters and his bowl," Hannah said.

"Can you bring your cell phone? I forgot mine at home."

Hannah dug into her beach bag and put on her t-shirt and shorts.

I took a deep breath. Finally, I could relax. She was contained.

We followed paw prints southward until they disappeared at the edge of the water. We both looked at the vanishing paw prints with discomfort.

"He knows how to swim," I said, more for my own benefit than Hannah's.

We kept walking.

After a while, Hannah said, "Can I ask you a personal question?"

"Sure," I answered as we trudged through the heat.

Hannah slowed her pace a bit and wiped her arm across her forehead. "Are you adopted?"

"What?" I hadn't been expecting *that* question. "No, why do you ask?" I answered casually, knowing *exactly* why she asked.

"Well, you, your Grandpa and Mom all have the last name Boyd, right?"

"Yes, that's because we're re-la-ted."

"And your grandfather is your mom's dad?

"Yeah."

"And well, you don't look very much like either one of them," she said hesitantly. "I mean, your mom has red hair and fair skin. Your grandfather's also light, and you're kind of… not."

"Olive. It's called an olive complexion. I've got dark eyes, dark hair, and I'm not pasty like my mom. It means I have more melanin in my skin. I don't burn easily." I looked at her. "Your complexion is darker than your mom's, too, but that doesn't make you adopted."

"Her people are Scandinavian." Hannah walked faster to catch up. "So, uh… I guess you look like your dad?"

I stopped abruptly and looked her straight in the eye (not the easiest thing for me to do). "I haven't gotten the results from the entire Human Genome Project, but I would guess, yes."

She nodded slightly.

"He's dead." I wasn't actually sure if that was true.

"He died before I was born." I think. It wasn't something Mom and I talked about. "He was tall and dark—you know, Mediterranean-looking." At that point I was just making stuff up.

"You're like Greek or Italian?" she asked.

"Yeah."

"Which one?"

"I don't know."

"Aren't you curious?"

I hated questions about my father. I was already dreading having to make a Punnett Square in freshman Biology.

And of course, it was all a lie.

In fifth grade, when I got interested in learning about DNA, I made a move toward learning about my father. I told Mom I needed my birth certificate so the guidance counselor could register me for middle school. I asked for my immunization records too, just to make it look legit. She disappeared into her bedroom and returned with a sealed (*sealed!*) manila envelope—like she kept a reserve of them in her bedroom.

She handed the envelope to me and said, "Just give it *directly* to your guidance counselor and make sure you don't open it."

"Why?" I asked.

"Well, I don't want you to lose it. It's my only copy. New ones cost 25 dollars."

Money was always an issue with my mom.

I tucked the envelope in my backpack. Later that day, I took it back to my room, locked the door, and had a long look at the proof that I existed. First thing I noticed was that my middle name was misspelled. Could my mother have taken just a few minutes to get my birth certificate correct?

Apparently not.

Then I skimmed down the page. The line next to *Father's Name* was blank, as was his place of birth and birth date. Either Mom didn't know *who* my father was, or he was someone so bad, that to me and the state of North Carolina, he was to remain anonymous. Both scenarios gave me plenty to talk about with Dr. Blanchard.

He said I should just ask Mom about my father. But I couldn't. I'd rather go on believing that my mom had known my father's identity and that he really had died before I was born, than to think she didn't even know whose name to put on my birth certificate.

Dr. Blanchard said Mom might not realize how much it bothered me to not know about my father. He said that if I didn't tell her I was curious, then I was being dishonest with her and myself. If I asked her about my father, then it could "open a dialogue" with my mother, and that would be "healthy."

Nope.

I liked the dialogue door closed nice and tight.

Closed doors were safe doors.

"Hank?" Hannah said. "Hello? Are you in there?"

Hannah was waving her hand in front of my face.

"Huh?"

"I just asked you if you've ever done one of those DNA tests to find out about your heritage?"

I stopped walking and looked at her. "You're brilliant!"

"Seriously? You live your life jacked-up on DNA and you've never thought of testing your own?"

"No," I answered, feeling like an idiot. "I had a complete brain fart on that."

"Well, get one of those kits. I think I heard on the radio that they're on sale."

"I will! That's a great idea." How had I not considered it?

Hannah turned quickly southward. "You hear that?"

"Barking." I smiled then yelled, "Chaucer—we're coming! Stay there!"

We ran toward the barking.

"Do you think that's him?" Hannah asked between breaths.

"I don't know." I puffed. "It doesn't sound exactly like him."

Finally, exhausted, we arrived at the barking dog. It was a black Labrador, not Chaucer.

"Excuse me, sir," I said to the man with the dog. "Have you seen a bloodhound come through here?"

"Are those the dogs with the long floppy ears—kind of red and black?"

"Yes," Hannah answered.

"I saw him a while back, headed south. Seemed like he was tracking something."

I looked at the sun in the sky. "Maybe I should go back for the boat? That way we won't have to walk back once we find him. He'll be exhausted if he's been running all this time." I pointed southward. "I'll meet up with you farther down the island. You take the waters and Chaucer's bowl. He'll be thirsty. I'll bring the rest of the stuff when I come back."

"What if I get lost? I don't know this place like you do." She looked around. "I don't know it at all."

"Just stick to the shore. If you get to the end of the island, wait for me. Keep the mainland in sight. I can run back to the boat in about thirty minutes."

"You think you can run *that* fast in the sand in *this* heat? It's gotta be ninety degrees, and we're probably two or three miles from the boat!"

I motioned with my arm. "Just keep heading south along the water. If you stick to the shore, you'll be fine."

Hannah took the phone from her pocket. "Okay, it's almost four-thirty now."

I ran back to the umbrella as fast as I could with the heat and my nagging groin injury. Hannah was right, it took a lot more than thirty minutes. I was exhausted and drenched in sweat when I got back to our stuff, threw it in *Crime Cat*, jumped in the water to cool off, then jumped back in the boat and headed south.

I mumbled to Chaucer as if we were telepathically connected. "If you're hot, go for a swim. It'll cool you down. Just don't drink the salt water. You know better than that."

Motoring through the marsh, I envisioned the lacerating oyster beds, pinching crabs, and boat propellers that could hurt him. A sharp pain stabbed me behind my eye.

"Stop thinking about it!" I yelled at myself.

I hugged the shoreline as best I could and scanned the land, hoping to see Hannah or Chaucer, preferably both, together... safe. But I reached the southern tip of the island without finding either one.

16

It takes more energy to cool your body when it is hot than to warm your body when it is cold. Hot temperatures can deplete the human glucose resources the body needs to make decisions and solve problems. Research shows that warm temperatures can adversely affect decision-making skills. There's no Forensics 411 *episode about this, but you can Google it.*

MY HEART POUNDED in my ears. What was I thinking! I should've told her to stay right where she was. Had Hannah's bikini melted my brain cells?

After traveling the entire six-mile length, it was clear that Hannah and Chaucer weren't on the marsh side of the island. I needed to search the ocean-side. One choice was to fight my way through breakers in the inlet, then take the boat along the beach. That would mean negotiating the big waves in my small boat. I sat in the boat on the marsh side of the island, drank a bottle of water and watched the inlet waters churn, trying to decide if I could take on the incoming tide without capsizing.

The answer was no, *Crime Cat* couldn't handle the inlet. I beached her on the marsh side of the island, stuffed Hannah's bag with the remaining waters and food, and trekked toward the ocean side.

As I melted in the heat of the late afternoon sun, my heart began to race. I broke out in a sweat, but it was a different kind than what came with the ninety-degree temperature. It was a sweat that started deep inside me and worked its way to the surface. Next came the ache in my left arm, then the tingling in my hands. A freaking attack!

"No!" I reached for my stress foam in my pocket, but I was wearing my bathing suit. No pockets.

I looked at my surroundings, and suddenly I was falling backward into a tunnel. The sounds around me faded, and I felt like I was watching a silent movie of the seagulls and crashing waves. I breathed deeply and counted "*Uno, dos, tres, cuatro...*" until my heart slowed. It was one of Dr. Blanchard's techniques.

When I reached *cincuenta*, I called out their names, then started again with *uno*.

After a minute or two of counting, breathing, aching, and tingling, the tunneled shroud of silence began to lift. My hot skin turned clammy.

I took a deep breath.

It was over.

Mom would get home from work. Soon she would realize that something was wrong. She'd panic, then call the police, same as last time.

The sun slowly slumped behind the tallest pines on the mainland. Once it disappeared, I would have no means of finding my way in the dark. I kept calling for Hannah and Chaucer as I approached the six monstrous dunes, nicknamed "The Devil's Backbone." They formed a ridge along the interior of the island. I headed inland toward them so I could get a better view of the area before it got dark.

I climbed the tallest dune, which towered thirty or so feet above the rest of the island, and scanned for Hannah, Chaucer, and an exposed area where the wind off the water would be cooler and help to keep the no-see-ums and mosquitos at bay. That'd be where I slept.

I used my remaining energy to raise myself and push the sound of Hannah's name through my dry, chafed throat.

With no response, I sat down at the top of the dune and buried my face in my hands. My shoulders shook as silent tears dripped from my eyes. They mixed with the sweat and sunscreen on my face, forming a gritty paste that felt like sandpaper raking across my cheek as I wiped it away.

I allowed myself sixty seconds of self-pity and then pulled my body up to survey the island again. The breeze was dying down, which meant the no-see-ums and mosquitos would soon be out, hunting for prey. We were running out of time.

Without the wind, hearing was easier. A sound floated toward me. My heart jumped. It was faint, but I heard something.

"Hannah?" I called. "Chaucer?"

Did I hear the word "trees"?

"Hannah!" I yelled as loudly as I could, moving toward a clump of scrub oaks to the west. The soft sand swallowed my feet. I repeatedly stopped, called her name, listened, then followed the sound of the faint voice… if it was a voice.

I found her under a cluster of trees. Her face was red and puffy, but she looked glad to see me.

"Oh my gosh! What happened? You look awful!" I said.

"Well, I feel abhorrent, so I guess *awful* is your being nice," Hannah answered in a parched voice.

I smiled, relieved to know that she felt well enough to talk vocabulary. "Word of the day?" I asked.

She silently nodded as she scratched her arms, wincing with each movement.

"What happened? How did you get here?"

She took a deep breath. "I was walking along the water like you told me. I heard barking. I think it was Chaucer. I ran towards the sound, but then I saw the tall dunes and figured I'd be able to see better from up there. Only I tripped and fell. I hurt my ankle. And I'm so freaking itchy!"

I glanced at her swollen ankle.

She sniffled. "I dragged myself under the trees to get out of the sun. But the bugs are eating me up, and I lost the cell phone. It must've fallen out of my pocket, but I didn't realize it until I had pulled myself under here. My ankle hurt so much that I couldn't climb back to the dunes to look for it. I think I'm dying."

"Okay. I'll look for the cell phone." I glanced toward the dunes. "But first you need to drink some water." I removed the cap and handed her a bottle.

"Stay here. I'll be back." Then I turned back around to reassure her. "And you're not going to die! People hardly ever die of broken bones. Dehydration is a far greater threat at this point."

"You're a ray of sunshine!" she said.

I climbed through the sand and up the tallest dune. It was nearly dark, so I crawled on my hands and knees trying to feel for Hannah's cell phone. At the top of the dune, I spotted a set of flashing red lights. They were moving slowly south along the marsh side of the island. I waved my arms furiously. "Hey, we're over here!" I yelled.

They were too far away to see or hear me. My best bet was to find the cell phone and call 911.

I got back on my knees and felt around in the parts of the dune that I hadn't yet searched. I groped through the sand at the top of the dune, not sure if it was even the right dune. She could've fallen on any of them.

The red lights moved southward with a bright spotlight aimed at the shoreline.

I crawled through the sand.

Nothing.

I moved to the next dune closest to Hannah. It must have been thirty yards wide. I started at the bottom and worked my way to the top. My hand touched a large tree branch that could've caused Hannah's fall. If she were coming down the dune and tripped over the limb, then the phone would've fallen lower. I turned around and searched the area at the bottom of the dune again.

"Hurry!" Hannah growled.

"I'm trying. Do you know which dune you fell down?" I called back to her.

"The tall sandy one!" she answered in an impatient, faltering voice.

Just then, I felt smooth metal. I examined it with my hand, and my heart sank as I realized it was Chaucer's water bowl.

"Stop thinking about it! Find the cell phone!"

And I did. Just like that. For once, my self-talk worked.

I yelled to Hannah, "I've got the phone! I'm gonna go to the top of the dune and call for help."

17

A person does not have to be gone for 24 hours to be considered missing. Any person who has concern for the safety of another can report them missing at any time. Episode 5 of Forensics 411, *"Missing," examines the ins and outs of missing persons and NamUs, the National Missing and Unidentified Persons System.*

AFTER EXPLAINING who and where I was, the 911 operator transferred me to a conference call with a rescuer named Chad. He beached the rescue boat, and I watched as their spotlight slowly crossed the island.

"They're taking one step, now two," I yelled to Hannah. "ETA, time immemorial."

In the darkness, I heard a thud. "That was meant to hit you! How 'bout you shut up until you have good news!" Hannah yelled with her scratchy voice.

"Right," I answered with a nod, willing myself to for once, say the right thing.

I returned to find Hannah curled in a ball, shaking as if she were cold. I awkwardly patted her leg. "Don't worry. It's going to be okay. They're on the way."

"Do you think you could *not* touch my mangled ankle? It hurts!"

I snatched my hand away.

I scooted away and didn't bother her anymore.

What seemed like hours later, the rescuers arrived with our moms.

"Oh my God!" Mrs. Simmons said, bending over Hannah. She turned to glare at me with ice blue eyes. "What's wrong with her? Why's she all red and swollen?"

I started to tell Mrs. Simmons about the bugs, but the one with Chad embroidered on his shirt stepped forward. "Ma'am, can I have a look?"

"Yes," Mrs. Simmons answered.

"It looks like she has a lot of insect bites. The no-see-ums are vicious this time of year, especially when there's not much wind." He looked up at the trees. "Plus, they gravitate to vegetation."

In the meanwhile, Mom came over to hug me. "You scared the crap out of me!" She hugged me tight and mumbled, "I thought I'd lost you again." Then she pulled herself away and looked at me. "What happened to your nose?"

"Nothing. It's fine," I answered. "I... um... ran into a branch in the dark."

Chad had revived Hannah. "What happened?" Her eyes widened.

The rescuers tended to Hannah. They got her on a stretcher and gave her a shot to help with the itching and swelling of the bug bites. The other two rescuers came over and asked if they could look at me.

I lashed out, "I'm fine! Hannah's the one that needs your help. And Chaucer, he's out there somewhere. He hasn't had any water." I sniffled. "He might be dead. I've got to find him!" I turned away from the rescuers, aimed northward and moved out, like a soldier on a mission.

"Oh no, you don't!" Mom said as she grabbed my shirt and

pulled me backward. "It's dark. There's no way I'm going to let you wander around this island at night!"

"I need to find Chaucer!"

"Look, kid," the one named Jimmy said. "We need to get the girl to a hospital. Let's get you back home, and we'll come back at daybreak to look for your dog."

Chad interrupted, "Jimmy you know we can't do that."

Jimmy put his hand up. "It's okay. You don't have to be any part of it."

"Don't you guys have an extra spotlight we could use to find him?" I looked to my mom for agreement.

"I'm sorry Sweetie, tomorrow is the best they can do," Mom said. "You've been in the sun all day. You must be ready to drop. You'll be more help to Chaucer if you come back tomorrow, rested."

I argued. Mom put her hands on my shoulders. "I'm sorry. I know how much you love him. I do, too, but we just don't have a choice. We've got to take care of Hannah."

Hannah motioned for me to come to her on the stretcher. With her swollen hand, she reached out for mine and pulled me down so she could talk into my ear. "I know I heard him. He was a little bit north of here. He's out there, and you're going to find him. When you do, give him a big kiss, and tell him that I'll see him soon. Okay?" She squeezed my hand.

I nodded, not knowing what to say. In a few short weeks, I had made my first friend, and then she nearly died because of me. Why did my life go like that?

"It's okay," she whispered. Her puffy eyes started to droop. I guessed that was the medicine for the bug bites working. Unlike me, she would sleep well.

Chad handed me a spotlight and returned Mom and me to my boat. We motored home in silence.

Jimmy promised to meet me at the boat ramp at six-fifteen the next morning; together, we would find Chaucer.

18

Heatstroke is when a body becomes extremely overheated because of prolonged exposure to hot temperatures or physical exertion. Untreated heatstroke can quickly damage the brain, heart, kidneys, and muscles. A delay in treatment can make the damage worse. This increases the risk of serious complications or death. See Forensics 411 *episode 39, "When Mother Nature Kills."*

THE NEXT MORNING, Jimmy and Chad were both at the boat ramp. On the way to the island, Jimmy showed me his two-way radio and explained how the GPS worked. "We both have one of these to communicate." He pushed a button and two different colored lights blinked on the screen. "I'm the blue light, and Chad is yellow. As you can see, the lights are right on top of each other since we're here together."

Chad dropped Jimmy on the ocean side of Pelican Island. He waded ashore, then Chad and I went back to the marsh side. Before he anchored the boat, I jumped in the water. Impatiently, I watched as he unloaded the stretcher and a medical bag in slow motion. *Wasn't he trained to work quickly?*

"I'm going to need you to help me carry the stretcher," he said. "And you have got to do what I tell you, understand?"

"Yes," I answered. "Can we just get going before it gets too hot?"

"All right, let's head back to the trees where we found the girl last night."

"Hannah told me that she heard him crying north of The Devil's Backbone. We already know he's not at the trees."

"He wasn't there last night. Returning there will help us get our bearings. We're going to do things my way. Agreed?" Chad said.

"Fine," I answered, lowering my head.

"Look, we're not authorized to use the rescue vehicles to search for a *dog*. We're trying to help, but if our supervisor heard that we used county-owned equipment to do this, we could be in deep trouble. I'm the squad leader, and I'd lose my job."

"Oh... I didn't realize that."

Chad patted me on the shoulder. "It's okay. I really do want to help, but we need to get it done quickly."

"Nobody wants to find him faster than I do."

We trudged through the sand as the sun baked the island. We were close to the trees when the radio crackled.

"This is Jimmy. Do you read me?"

"Roger that, Jimmy."

"I found the dog. He's in bad shape. Bring the stretcher. I'm about a quarter mile due-north of the northern-most dunes of The Devil's Backbone. Can you locate me on GPS?"

Chad examined the walkie-talkie screen.

I checked over his shoulder to see the blue light on the screen.

"Roger that," Chad answered.

By the time he finished his sentence, I had dropped my end of the stretcher and taken off in a run in the direction of Jimmy's blue light.

"Get back here!" Chad yelled. "You need to stay with me!"

I ran faster. Chaucer was in bad shape. He needed me.

When I could run no farther through the deep loose sand, I stopped and caught my breath. I surveyed my surroundings.

Chad caught up to me dragging the stretcher. Breathing heavily, he grabbed me by my t-shirt. "You *promised* you were going to cooperate."

"But you heard Jimmy—Chaucer needs me."

Tight-lipped, Chad said, "He needs a doctor. If we lose *you*, then we're obligated to search for you instead, and your dog will never get the help he needs. Is *that* what you want?"

I shook my head.

Chad let go of my shirt. "Then stay with me. Got it?"

I nodded slightly.

When we reached the giant dunes, I spotted them. Jimmy was on his knees with his back facing me.

"Is he okay?" I asked.

Chaucer lay on his side panting violently. His closed eyes were swollen just like Hannah's. Blood covered his paws, front legs, and his nose.

"Why's he bleeding?" I asked.

"It looks like he's been digging. I came across several holes. Maybe he was trying to dig one to get cool. There's a huge pile of sand on the other side of the dune." He pointed without taking his eyes off Chaucer. "He could've cut them on shells or briars or maybe in the water on oyster beds."

"Might be DIC," Chad said, saying the letters as "dee eye see."

"What's that?" I asked.

"Nothing," Jimmy answered.

I bent down to stroke Chaucer's ears. They were hot enough to burst into flames, like ants under a magnifying glass.

Softly I said, "Chaucer, it's me." A tear rolled down my nose onto his.

"Look there! His tail just moved a little bit," Jimmy exclaimed.

"That's right. It's me. We're gonna get you to the doctor. Just hang on, okay?"

I willed his eyes to open and make contact with mine, and one opened a tiny bit.

"Keep talking to him while we get him loaded on the stretcher, okay? We need him to stay calm," Jimmy said.

The rescuers slowly slid the stretcher underneath Chaucer as I talked to him. His one open eye, filled with fear, never left mine.

Chaucer groaned when they lifted the stretcher, and a look of panic flashed across his face.

"It's okay. We're going to get you some help. Don't leave me." I had difficulty getting my words out.

"We need to get him to a veterinarian," Jimmy said.

I followed beside the stretcher, my hand resting on Chaucer's side. As we walked, I got a look at his shredded paws, caked with sand and blood.

We continued in silence until we reached the rescue boat, all of us out of breath and dripping sweat.

"Okay kid, you hop on the boat and go to the stern. We'll carry the stretcher back there and hoist it up. Just be there to talk to him while we raise him up over the side of the boat. We don't want him getting spooked and try to jump off."

We got Chaucer settled on the deck of the boat. Jimmy handed me a cold pack. "Hold it on the bottom of his paws. The pads are one of the main places that dogs release heat from their body. We need to get his body temp down."

I nodded.

"I'll call ahead to Doc Taylor and let him know that we've got a bloodhound coming in with dehydration and possible heat stroke," Chad said.

I yelled over the roar of the boat engine. "Tell him it's Chaucer! Doc Taylor knows him."

19

Humans first domesticated dogs 12,000–15,000 years ago. Dogs can understand both verbal and body signals from humans better than any other species. A dog bonded to its human can often sense their owner's emotional state by the tone of his voice. See **Forensics 411** *episode 6, "Sniffing Out Crime."*

Doc Taylor and his assistant were waiting at the entrance to the clinic. They loaded the stretcher onto a gurney and wheeled Chaucer into the building.

"Does your mom or grandpa know you're here?" the assistant asked.

"No," I answered. I hadn't even thought of them.

"We're going to take Chaucer back and work on him. You need to get one of them over here."

"Okay." I nodded.

When I approached the lobby desk, Miss Danielle, the office manager, said, "I just called your mom; she's on her way." Miss Danielle and my mom were high school friends, and her daughter Katelyn was in my grade.

I sat in the corner of the lobby and dialed Hannah's number.

No one answered, so I left a message. "Hannah, we found Chaucer. He's alive... but just barely. They're working on him right now. Um... I hope you're feeling better. I'm sorry about everything. Really."

I leaned back, wishing for my piece of foam to squeeze away the misery. I waited for Hannah to call back. I waited for my mom to show up. I waited for Doc Taylor to come out and tell me about Chaucer.

A while later, Mom burst through the door and headed straight to Danielle without noticing me in the corner.

"Is he okay?" Mom asked.

I looked up as Danielle pointed toward me. Mom's heels clicked across the floor. "Sweetie? How is he?"

I jumped up and let her swallow me in her arms. "He's bad. They have him in the back."

"It's okay. He's in good hands. Doc Taylor will do everything he can."

I tried to hide my tears inside Mom's hug. She whispered, "Did you take your medicine today?"

"Yes," I mumbled. Was she asking me about my medicine because she thought Chaucer was going to die? Did she think a pill could fix that?

Nothing could fix that.

As we sat down on a bench, I closed my eyes and tried not to think about what could happen to Chaucer.

It was another hour before Doc Taylor came out to talk with us.

"How is he?" I asked.

"He's severely dehydrated and has heat stroke. His temperature was higher than our thermometers go. We wiped him down with cool water, applied ice packs all over his body, and passed a urinary catheter. That drained out his warm urine and we infused him with cold IV fluids to help get his temperature down from the inside out. We'll be monitoring his blood work for signs of DIC."

"What's that?" I asked. The rescuers had mentioned those same letters.

"Well," Doc Taylor said, "It's something we don't want."

"Tell me. He's my dog—my responsibility. I need to know."

"DIC is when the body gets so hot that it essentially starts to cook itself."

Mom and I gasped.

Doc Taylor put his hands up. "It's okay. I think you got to him soon enough. I'll keep doing blood work to make sure his proteins are in balance—that's the first chemical sign of DIC. In the meanwhile, we're giving him tons of cold IV fluids and alcohol rubs. His temp is down to 103.7."

"Normal is 101, right?" I asked.

"Yes," he answered. "We're also giving him IV antibiotics. I think he cut his paws digging, but we're having trouble getting the bleeding to stop. Heat stroke can mess with the blood's ability to clot."

I nodded, wishing I hadn't read so many accounts of victims bleeding to death. It was a horrible way to die.

"Did you notice how his nose was cut and scraped?" Doc Taylor asked. "It's something I've seen in search and rescue dogs. They are trained to find a missing person and if they aren't successful or they find a person that's not alive, they go crazy."

My heart sank. "I've been working with him a little bit on following a scent, but nothing serious. Did I cause this?"

"Oh, Sweetie, no," Mom answered. "This was an accident. It wasn't your fault." She squeezed my shoulder.

"Is he going to be okay?" Mom asked.

"I hope so," answered Doc Taylor.

That was different than I *think so.*

"We've dressed the pads of his feet. Once we get the bleeding to stop, we'll glue them. He'll need to stay here for a few days, so we can continue to monitor his blood chemistry and give him fluids."

Doc Taylor studied me. "Do you want to go back and see him?"

CHAUCER WAS LYING ON A GURNEY. The sight of him put a lump in my throat.

"Hey boy, are you okay? You scared me to death."

Chaucer's eyes, cloaked in exhaustion, didn't respond. I kissed him on the head and tousled his ears. "I'm so sorry you got hurt." I buried my head in the black fur on his side.

A small whimper escaped from his throat.

"Don't talk. Save your strength, okay? You've got to rest up. Doc Taylor is going to take good care of you. I'll be right outside, and I'll check on you again in a little bit."

I lay my head where I thought his heart was and said, "Promise me you won't die. Please don't leave me."

20

Research shows that when investigators interview witnesses or suspects, right-handed people usually look up and to the right if they are lying about something they saw. Police use this to help them decide whether a witness or suspect is speaking truthfully. See Episode 21 of Forensics 411, *"Those Lying Eyes."*

WHILE CHAUCER WAS in the hospital, I visited him every chance I got and texted Hannah with updates. She didn't respond to any of them. It had been four days since the island, and I worried that the inevitable end of our friendship had come.

By contrast, I couldn't get rid of Dillon the Villain. He was not happy about being banned from the pool, so he kept sending me threatening texts. As I said, harassing me (some would say stalking) was a sport for him. Menacing texts during the summer was his version of off-season conditioning. His favorite text message to me was Your going down crime kid!

I rolled my eyes at his stupidity and texted back: It's YOU'RE not YOUR. Why not use this summer to master your homophones?

Immediately, he responded with: The only homo around hear is you!

"Here" with an "a"? *Are you kidding me?*

As I raised my finger to my phone, prepared to teach Dillon a thing or two about spelling, I heard Dr. B whisper in my ear: "Do not engage."

Doc Taylor came out to the waiting room where I sat. "You know you can go home. I promise we'll take good care of him."

"If he's here, I'm here."

"Well, I don't have any appointments for another two hours and was going to go get some lunch. You want to tag along? My treat."

"Sure."

It was the perfect opportunity to question the former custodian of Vista Point High about Stacy McFarland.

WE WALKED JUST DOWN the street to the Corner Café.

"This okay?" he asked.

"Yes, thank you," I answered. We sat at a table near a window and ordered sweet tea.

I pretended to look at the menu as I planned how to work Doc Taylor's former employment into the conversation.

"Did you grow up in Vista Point?" I asked.

"Sure did. Graduated from Vista Point High in 1983."

"Where did you go to college?"

"North Carolina A&M, then vet school at the Veterinary Medical College of North Carolina."

"So, you graduated from college in what, 1987?"

"Well, no. My family didn't have the money for me to go to college right out of high school. We had to save up."

"Yeah, I'm worried my mom won't be able to pay for my college. I hope I can get a scholarship," I said. "Did you get one?"

"Well, I got lucky. I worked a couple of years after high school, then I got some financial help. I guess you could call it a scholarship."

"Oh really? What kind did you get?"

"My father's employer knew that I had excellent grades in high school but couldn't afford to go to college. He offered to help me out."

"Where did your dad work?" I asked.

"Buckley Motors. He was a mechanic."

I nodded calmly, but inside my brain was enjoying an explosion of pyrotechnics. We had a connection between Doc Taylor and the Buckleys!

"That was really nice. Where'd you work before you got your scholarship?"

"At the high school." He cleared his throat. "I was... um... a custodian."

"Really?" I tried to sound surprised.

At that moment, the waitress came to take our order. Then I resumed my questions.

"Wow, that's pretty cool to have gone from being a custodian to a doctor."

"Yes," Doc Taylor said. "I guess I got lucky."

I went in for the kill. "Did you work at the school when that girl, Stacy McFarland, disappeared?"

I watched Doc Taylor swallow hard. "Who?"

"Stacy McFarland. She was a girl who lived in my neighborhood. She would have been a student when you were a custodian. Someone robbed her house back in 1985, and she vanished. The police said she robbed it herself and ran away."

He blushed and then nodded slowly. "Oh, right, I remember. That was a long time ago. Why do you ask?"

"I've got a web show called *Forensics 411*, and I'm making an episode about her disappearance. If you get a chance, like me on Facebook, Instagram, Twitter, and YouTube. It would really help me out."

He chuckled and said he would, looking more relaxed.

I cut to the point. "Were you the one who found the journal in her locker?"

He hesitated. "Journal?"

"Stacy's journal."

"I, uh… why do you ask?"

I could tell I was getting under his skin, which I hated to do because Doc Taylor was always so kind to Chaucer and me. I mean seriously, the guy was buying me lunch.

"It was a key piece of evidence in the McFarland case, and the cops lost it."

He nodded. "Yeah, I remember that, now that you mention it."

"What a coincidence that you worked at the school during the time of her disappearance. I mean, being a custodian, you must have known everything that went on there. Do you remember seeing her journal in her locker? That's where the cops said they found it."

Doc Taylor looked over his shoulder in both directions and then leaned in toward me, lowering his voice. "Why do you ask?"

"For my web show," I answered. "I think the cops may have made a mistake."

He shifted around in his seat uncomfortably.

In good-cop mode, I said, "Doc Taylor, I need an honest answer."

He said, "I don't know what you mean," but his eyes told me a different story. Dr. B says eyes don't lie.

"During the time you were a custodian at Vista Point High, was it your job to clean out the lockers after school let out?"

"Sort of," he answered. "The teachers always had the kids take everything out of their lockers a few days before school ended. As soon as school was over, I'd wipe each locker out and reset the combination. They'd leave the doors open…" He stopped talking mid-sentence.

"So, is it fair to say that if anything, such as a journal, was left in Stacy McFarland's locker, that you would have seen it in June when school let out?"

He nodded slightly, understanding my line of questions.

I looked him straight in the eye. "Is it possible that someone from the police department, or maybe from the Buckley family, came to you and asked you to say that you found a journal in Stacy's locker when you hadn't?"

He looked down.

"And did you agree to say that you found the journal in exchange for a loan or scholarship to college?"

"No! Absolutely not," he answered in a whisper. Then he leaned across the table toward me. "He came with the scholarship first—*before* he said anything about the journal. It wasn't my idea. I never volunteered to lie. I thought Old Man Buckley was just being generous with the scholarship."

I leaned farther in towards the center of the table. "So, Bob Buckley Sr. came to you with the offer?"

He whispered, "Actually he went to my father."

"Did your parents know the reason Bob Sr. offered to help you pay for college?"

"Are you kidding? They didn't know anything. At the time, *none* of us did. My parents and I believed Mr. Buckley saw a lot of potential in me and was just being generous. After that, Dad thought Mr. Buckley walked on water. He agreed to accept the scholarship and loan *before* Bob Sr. came to me about the journal. When he asked me to go along with the story that the journal had been in Stacy's locker, my dad had already accepted the financial help. I couldn't say 'no.' And I never told my parents."

"I didn't mean to hurt anyone. Really. When the cops held the press conference, Mayor Buckley—he was the investigating cop back then—didn't say who found the journal. All I had to do was stand behind the cops during the press conference and *look* like I found it. If anyone questioned me, I was supposed to say that I must have missed it when I was cleaning out the lockers earlier in the summer." He shrugged. "That was true. I never saw that journal in any locker."

"Are you sure?"

"I'm positive. I always took anything I found in lockers or the hallways to the main office. The only time I ever saw that journal was at the press conference."

"Did you look in it?"

"No. I never touched it. I saw Bob Jr. holding it up to show the press. It just looked like a spiral notebook to me."

"Did he open it for the press?"

"I honestly don't remember. All I wanted to do was get out of there."

"You've never told anyone that the cops fabricated the journal?"

"Nope. And I can't say for sure that they did. Maybe Bob Jr. didn't have a search warrant for the place that he found the journal; so, he put it in the locker to cover his tracks. I've seen that on TV."

"Do you think Bob Jr. felt a lot of pressure to solve the case?" I asked.

"Of course. It's a small town. Vista Point had never had a case like that before. Everyone was scared for their kids. For all we knew, the McFarland girl could've been the first of a bunch of serial killings or kidnappings."

"So, if the journal revealed that Stacy was miserable and planning to run away, that would put the town's fears at ease and give the cops reason to say they'd solved the case."

Doc Taylor nodded. "It did calm the town down once they closed the case."

Our food came, and we ate in silence for a few minutes.

"Do *you* think Stacy McFarland ran away?" I asked.

"I don't know. I never knew her personally, but the teachers at school said they couldn't picture her being the type to run away from home. Her parents offered a 50 thousand dollar reward, and her picture was on milk cartons and stuff." He shrugged. "All I know is that there was something fishy about that journal, and I was too much of a coward to say anything."

21

Dogs trained in Human Remains Detection (HRD), also known as cadaver dogs, can detect skin, hair, teeth, and skeletal remains that are hundreds of years old. See Forensics 411 episode 6, "Sniffing Out Crime."

AFTER DAYS of Hannah ignoring my texts, I broke down and called her. I wasn't going to let her go without a fight.

To my relief, she answered. "Oh, hey. What's up?"

I mustered the courage to ask a direct question. It wasn't easy for me. If it were, I might actually know who my father was.

"Are you mad at me?" I asked.

"No. Why would I be mad at you?"

"You haven't been answering my texts."

"My mom took my phone. My ankle's barely sprained, but she has me under house arrest. It's killing me—not my ankle, but Mom's protectiveness. It's not like texting is going to suppress my immune system. I just got my phone back a few minutes ago."

I did a tiny fist pump.

"I have a ton of McFarland-related stuff to tell you. And Chaucer's coming home from the hospital tomorrow. Do you want to go with me and my mom to get him?"

"Absolutely. I miss that big guy."

We caught up on things like I imagined friends did when they hadn't talked for a few days and made plans for the following day.

WHEN WE WALKED through the front door with Chaucer, Grandpa was in the kitchen, sporting a wool sweater and Bermuda shorts, seemingly unaware that it was ninety-four degrees outside.

"What's that good-for-nothing dog wearing on his head?" he asked.

"It's a surgical collar," I answered, "to keep him from chewing his paws."

"Well, he looks like a sissy!" Grandpa answered back. "Why are his feet all wrapped up? Is he doing ballet now?"

"He tore them up on Pelican Island. *Remember?* The doctor thinks maybe he was tracking a scent."

"That damn dog couldn't track his food bowl if you set it in front of him," Grandpa said as he dismissed us with a wave of his hand.

I pointed Chaucer toward the crate. "Come on boy, you have to go in. Doctor's orders." He whined and stubbornly dug his paws in, refusing to move.

"It's okay Chaucer," Hannah said, rubbing his ears. "I hurt one of my paws on the island too, and I had to stay in bed for a few days. But look at me now, I'm all better."

I pulled him by the collar into his crate and closed the door. "*Quick*—outside!"

I said to Hannah. "He's a master of manipulation. Don't make eye contact."

We scurried out to the back porch just as he started to whine.

"Thanks for helping," I said as we sat on the top step of the porch. "I think he was glad to see you."

"Well, I'm happy he's getting better. I was worried about him."

I hesitated, unsure how to say what I needed to say.

"Look, I'm really sorry about everything that happened on Pelican Island. I didn't mean for you to get lost or hurt. It was great of you to go after him like that. I don't think he'd be alive if you hadn't heard him."

"Do you think he was tracking something like the vet said?"

"I don't know. Chaucer's been on that island a hundred times. He's never disappeared like that. I didn't get a glimpse of the hole the rescuer said he dug, but I'm gonna go back and check it out."

"I wish I could go too, but my mom said I'm not allowed to go back out on the boat with you. *Ever.* She says that what happened made her realize that fourteen is too young to go sailing off to an island without grown-ups."

"It's not like we went to Bermuda or something. We went *one* mile across the waterway. We never lost sight of land or got out of cell phone range."

"I made those arguments, but Mom's got me on maritime lockdown."

"Well, I'm going back over there as soon as I can. But first, let me tell you what I found out from Doc Taylor about Stacy's journal."

Hannah and I sat on the back porch most of the evening talking about what I had learned from Doc Taylor.

"Clearly, the Buckleys wanted that case closed," I said.

"Did they want the case closed so bad that they lied about the journal? And if so, why?" Hannah asked.

"I don't know. I don't see Mayor Buckley as the type to want to quell the town's fears about a serial killer so selflessly."

"But look at it this way," Hannah said, "If Bob Buckley solved the case, he helped himself. He would seem like a great investigator, which we know he wasn't. Saying Stacy ran away put Vista Point's mind at ease, and he became a hero."

"*And* got the McFarlands off his back," I added.

22

I *t is a misconception that bones don't decompose. They do, but at a much slower rate than other tissues. Several environmental issues, such as humidity, soil type, and ambient temperature can affect the rate of decomposition. See* **Forensics 411** *Episode 8, "Breaking Down the Decomposition Process."*

THE NEXT DAY I beached *Crime Cat* on the marsh side of Pelican Island across from The Devil's Backbone. The path from the shore to the large central dunes was a grueling and gradual uphill trek through mounds of loose sand. In fact, it wasn't a path at all. I used my shovel as a sickle to hack my way through the tall grasses and prickly briars that guarded the dunes.

As I approached The Devil's Backbone, I spotted the mounds of displaced sand Chaucer had nearly died excavating. I approached it slowly, allowing my imagination to sort out all the possible things he could've unearthed.

I cautiously peeked beyond the edge of the hole. The truth was more surprising than anything I could have imagined.

At the bottom of the hole was a skull! A skinless, hairless, human skull!

I wrestled my phone out of my pocket, took three pictures, then started digging away at the side of the hole with my hands. The skull lay about four feet below. The excitement pumping through my veins must have been what Chaucer felt when he discovered the same bones.

"Wait—get a grip, detective! You know the protocol. You can't just start digging." This was most likely a crime scene, and I didn't want to destroy evidence. People didn't usually bury themselves.

I paused, not wanting to listen to the rational voice urging me to turn these findings over to Chief Buckley, with his delusions of adequacy. I wanted to pick up the skull and examine it for cracks; to measure the mandible to see if it belonged to a male or female. If I had the equipment to identify it right there on the island, I'd be the kid who was famous for discovering a dead body. That would definitely get me more followers!

I considered what I knew. It took a *minimum* of a year for hair and skin to decompose. Since the body was deep in the sand, which had a much lower acidity than soil, the decomposition process would have been slower than if buried in regular dirt. The bones had probably been there for years.

I ran back to the boat as fast as my legs would carry me. When I got there and caught my breath, I called Hannah.

"Hey," she chirped. "Did you find something on the island?"

"Get up to my house right now! You don't want to miss this!"

"I'm just on my way home from… an appointment, but I'll be there as soon as I can," she said.

WHEN I GOT BACK HOME, Mom was in the backyard pulling weeds. I took a deep breath and spilled the truth. "I went back to Pelican Island this morning because I wanted to see what Chaucer had been digging for, and this is what I found!" I shoved the phone toward her.

She backed up a little, so she could focus on the photo, then gasped. "Is that a skull?"

"Yes!" I answered. "Chaucer dug it up on Pelican Island. That's how he tore up his paws. I think Doc Taylor was right. He has instincts for searching."

"Was there a whole skeleton, or just a skull?" Mom asked as she took off her gardening gloves and set them on the steps of the porch.

"I think a whole body. I didn't want to disturb the scene." *A lie if ever I told one.* "I thought I saw a hand. We need to call the police before somebody else finds it and contaminates the site."

"Where is it exactly?"

"The north end of The Devil's Backbone."

Mom called the police, who said they would send over an officer. Immediately after she hung up, the doorbell rang.

"That was fast!" Mom said.

"That's probably Hannah," I said as I ran to the door.

Hannah limped in and said, "Argh. Did ye find some treasure, laddie?"

"Nope, but I found this!" I pushed the phone into her hand.

"That's a skull!"

"A human skull," I said with a smile.

At that moment, the doorbell rang again.

"Who keeps ringing the damn bell?" Grandpa yelled from the den. "I'm trying to bid on some bagpipes!"

"I bet that's the police," Mom said.

"The police?" Grandpa yelled back. "Did you wreck the car again, Angela?"

My mom shook her head and yelled back over her shoulder as she stepped to the front door. "No Dad! I haven't wrecked my car since I was in high school. Stay off eBay! You don't need any more bagpipes!"

Mom glared at me. "Did you change the password like I told you?"

"*Yes*, but he keeps changing it back. He's surprisingly savvy on the computer."

Mom opened the door. "Ms. Boyd?" asked the tall dark-haired officer.

"Yes, please come in." She motioned for him to enter.

"I'm Officer Steve Corker. I received a call that your son found a skull."

"Yes, out on Pelican Island," I answered from behind Mom.

Mom motioned to me, "This is my son, Boom—"

"Hank," I said, cutting her off. "Hank Boyd." I could picture myself flashing an FBI badge.

"When did you start going by Hank?" Mom asked.

"Jiminy Cricket, Angela! Where you been?" Grandpa said from behind us. "The boy changed his name weeks ago!"

"Okay," Mom said. "I must've missed the memo on that one... *Hank*."

Hannah watched the whole thing and I cringed.

"Actually, my dog found it." I showed the officer the pictures on my phone.

"That really *is* a human skull!" the officer exclaimed. "I thought they were pulling my leg down at the station. I've just been with the Vista Point police for a few months, and the only violent crime I've had to deal with was a pedicure gone bad at the nail salon." He chuckled.

It's just like Chief Buckley to send a rookie.

"I didn't want to disturb the scene, so I just took some pictures, then headed back home to call the police."

"If you had the cell phone with you, why didn't you call from there?"

I looked at the cop. Good question. This rookie might be okay.

"I thought I should tell my mom about it and let her call. I wasn't sure they'd take a kid seriously. Plus, I knew I'd need to lead you to the skeleton. It's not easy to find." I looked down at my legs that had been stuck and bloodied by briars on the island.

"We'll need a boat to get over there. Let me call the station and tell the chief what's going on."

After making his call outside, Officer Corker came back in. "I spoke with Chief Buckley. He's going to head over there but needs to transfer equipment from the van to the department boat. He said that could take a bit."

"The chief didn't send you here?" Hannah asked Corker.

"No, I was just next in line to answer the call, but he sounded interested. We don't get many dead bodies around here."

"I can take you over in my boat."

"That would be great," he answered. "Is that okay with you, Ms. Boyd?"

My eyes pleaded with Mom.

"I bet my dad would go along to help." Without waiting for an answer, Hannah said, "I'll call him."

"Your dad?" I asked.

"Yeah. I already told you my mom said no more island for me. But she can't argue if Dad goes along."

Seconds later she hung up. "Mom wasn't home." Hannah smiled. "My dad'll be here in five minutes." Then her eyes got huge. "That could be Stacy McFarland! We might've solved the case!"

Grandpa piped in. "They still haven't found that girl? She's been missing for months!"

More like decades, but I never argued with Grandpa about such things. Time wasn't an exact science for him anymore.

Officer Corker's dark eyes widened. "Who's Stacy McFarland?"

Hannah explained before I could stop her. "She used to live on this street but disappeared in 1985. We've been investigating the case."

I coughed loudly and squeezed Hannah's arm so she would shut up. We didn't know if we could trust this guy.

The doorbell rang again.

"I bet that's my dad," Hannah said, running to the door as if it were her own.

She yanked the door open and yelled over her shoulder "Okay, it's my dad, let's head out."

As I filled my backpack with chilled water bottles, I glanced toward the door where Mr. Simmons stood. He was not what I expected—decked out in plaid Bermudas, a polo shirt and leather loafers.

23

C *rime scene investigators or technicians collect, protect, and* *preserve evidence. A crime scene technician must know how to expose, photograph, and remove fingerprints and other evidence using specialized light and chemical techniques. See* Forensics 411 *episode 4, "Tools of the Trade."*

MR. SIMMONS, obviously a fan of the preppy movement, chatted with Officer Corker the whole way to the Devil's Backbone while Hannah and I stared at the awkward wall of silence between us.

When we got there, Corker and Mr. Simmons wrapped the area in crime tape while I figured out how to formulate my question.

"You want some water?" I asked Hannah. I made sure I looked casual with my loose hips and unlocked knees.

"Sure." She walked over to me.

I began, still sending out casual body language. "So, um... your dad..."

She smoothed and tucked her insubordinate hair into its ponytail, tilted her head and arched her eyebrow. "What about him?"

"He's um, sort of...."

She tapped her foot in the sand and waited for me to find the right word. Where was Dr. Blanchard when I needed him?

"Um, his epidermis is darker than I expected."

"Yep. He has more melanin. It provides natural protection from the sun." She held back a smirk as she lobbed my own words at me.

"Why didn't you tell me?" I asked, immediately wishing I hadn't.

Had I accidentally sent out racist vibes that made her feel like she had to hide him from me?

"I never told you my mom was white, but you figured it out when you met her. You never told me your grandfather likes kilts, but I figured it out when I met him. I don't think my father's skin color has to be an issue and I hope you don't either."

"Well... no, it's not an issue. It was just ..."

"What?"

"A surprise," I answered.

Who was I to judge her dad? I didn't even know my father's name. But comparing my complexion to my mom's it seemed logical that my dad was a little on the brown side of beige himself.

"My dad is bi-racial. His father is black, and his mom is white. They live in Pittsburgh."

I studied those freakishly-light hazel eyes. I wanted to know more. Anything unexpected fascinated me. And it was easier to ask about her father than to question my own mother about mine.

But an in-depth look into her soul told me that now was not the time. So, I said, "Let me show you the body."

AT THE HOLE CHAUCER DUG, I studied the body as best I could without maneuvering it. Hannah hovered behind me.

"That looks like a hand," I told her. "The fingernails are gone. Nails are one of the last things to decompose. This body could have been here for years or decades," I whispered. "I wish I could tell if the body's wearing clothes."

"Gross," Hannah murmured.

"The clothing could tell us the gender and a rough age of the skeleton. If there are no clothes, then someone buried the body naked, or it's been here for at least ten years. Most natural fabrics disintegrate within ten years. Only durable fabrics, like canvas, take longer than that to decompose. And of course, some synthetic fabrics like polyester can take hundreds of years to biodegrade.

As I looked closer, I noticed a piece of sand-colored fabric.

"It looks like there's a piece of cloth under the skull," I said.

Corker came up behind us. "You didn't touch anything did you?"

"No, I was just trying to get a better look."

"I got a call from the chief," Officer Corker said. "The CSI unit is on its way. They're following my GPS signal and should be here in thirty minutes."

"What's taking them so long?" Hannah said. "It's been two hours since you called him."

"Vista Point has a CSI team?" I asked.

As Mr. Simmons took off his loafers and tossed them to the side, clearly realizing that they were a mistake, he addressed Officer Corker. "I'm new around here, but I went to college with the district attorney, Mark Ellis. I bet he would like to know there's a dead body in his jurisdiction. Have you contacted him?"

"I have to go through proper channels. The chief will assess the situation and contact the district attorney. I doubt he'd like me jumping the chain of command."

Officer Corker turned to me. "So, tell me more about this missing girl."

I elaborated only on the information that we gleaned from the newspaper clippings. Mr. Simmons listened intently, seeming as if he was trying to stifle a smile.

When I'd finished explaining the McFarland case, he patted Hannah on the shoulder and said, "If your Mom finds out about this, she's going to kill you." He shook his head. "Then she's gonna kill me!"

AN HOUR LATER, Chief Buckley arrived, gasping for air and dripping with sweat. "I hear we've got ourselves some bones." The overweight, balding man stuffed his escaping shirt back into his pants and used a handkerchief to wipe his forehead. Two brittle-looking unshaven men dressed in plain clothes followed.

"Yes, sir," Corker answered nervously.

I whispered to Hannah, "The CSI team must've been taken off an undercover job."

Hannah coughed. "Posing as garbage men, I think."

"And that one has obviously not seen a dentist in a while," I mumbled.

"Or a shower," Hannah added.

The chief addressed Corker. "Okey-dokey, little puppy, the big dogs are here. You can go on back to the porch and wait for us to come home." He patted Corker on the head.

"I've secured the scene," Corker answered with a red face. Pointing to me he added, "This is Hank Boyd. He's the one that found the body and called it in."

"Boyd?" The chief looked me up and down with disdain. "You Henry Boyd's grandson? They call you 'Tigger' or something, don't they?" He nodded. "That's right. A few years back you went mi—"

"Yes!" I interrupted. "Henry Boyd's my grandfather. I used to go by 'Boomer,' when I was younger."

He tried to beat me down with his silent glare, but I stood tall.

"Thanks for the call. We'll take it from here." The chief shooed us away.

The CSI men stood awkwardly behind Chief Buckley. Not only were they not wearing uniforms, but neither had a name tag. They only carried shovels. Where were their cameras, evidence bags, and measuring devices? Why had it taken them hours to load three shovels on the police department boat?

Hannah's dad offered his hand to the chief, "I'm John Simmons. The district attorney, is a friend of mine. Are you going to alert him that a body's been discovered?"

Chief Buckley didn't take Mr. Simmons' hand. "I don't need some Yankee-stranger telling me how to do my job!"

He turned to Corker. "How 'bout you escort these folks off the island, so the professionals can work. I assume you need to get home to change that filthy uniform. It's a disgrace to the department!"

"Um, yes sir," Corker said.

"I'm sure that Tigger here can give you a ride back in his little yacht," the chief chuckled.

I protested. "Don't you want to question me?"

He put his hand up. "No thanks. Get on home now."

Frustrated, we glanced at each other, then skulked away.

"What a jerk!" Hannah said as soon as we were out of earshot. "Can he seriously do that?"

"He just did," Mr. Simmons answered, running his hand across his closely cropped hair.

Soaked in sweat, Hannah said, "I think that body in the dunes could be Stacy, and I doubt that she ran away to Pelican Island and buried herself!"

Corker piped in, "It seems highly coincidental that you're researching a missing person case from 1985 and then boom, your dog happens to dig up her body."

"True, but that body has to be someone," I answered. "I scoured NamUs for unidentified bodies that might be Stacy and didn't find any. But that was a longshot anyway. That website isn't designed for the general public."

I turned to Corker and arched my eyebrow. "I bet you've got access to a lot of law enforcement databases."

"What's NamUs?" Mr. Simmons asked.

"That's the National Missing and Unidentified Persons System. It's sort of the lost and found of human remains," I answered.

Corker said, "Once the CSI team exhumes the body and gets it to the medical examiner, they'll be able to check the teeth, if there are any, and see if they match the McFarland girl's dental records."

"How long do you think it'll take for them to run whatever tests they need to identify the body?" Hannah asked.

"I can't imagine it would take more than a few days," Corker answered. "As long as they don't have trouble tracking down the parents, I think that the medical examiner should know whether that body is Stacy McFarland by early next week. So, check Tuesday's or Wednesday's paper. It'll be front page news."

Hannah asked, "Can you let us know when you find out the identity, rather than us having to wait for the paper? I mean, we *are* sort of insiders."

"I don't know," the officer answered. "I doubt that would make the chief happy."

"Could you check the databases that the states and feds keep on missing persons? Based on my knowledge of forensics and decomposition, that skeleton has been there at least ten years. If that's not Stacy McFarland, it's someone else who disappeared a long time ago."

"Sure, I can do that without raising any eyebrows," Corker answered. "Besides, you've got me curious about this McFarland girl."

24

A medical examiner is a doctor who determines cause and manner of death, time of death, supervises the collection of evidence from the body and identifies unknown corpses and skeletal remains. He may or may not be a trained forensic pathologist. A coroner can also determine cause and manner of death but is typically a sheriff or funeral director and does not have any medical training. Coroners are elected or appointed. For more information see Forensics 411 *episode 10, "Medical Examiners: A Cut Above."*

THE SKELETON we found on Pelican Island wasn't front-page news. In fact, it wasn't *any* page news. Not Sunday, Monday, or Tuesday. The *Vista Point Voice* headline that day informed concerned citizens that police charged someone in the theft of Mrs. Beverly Clatterbuck's weed-whacker.

"Thank God for that!" I said to Chaucer after reading the headline. "We might've had a serial landscaper on our hands."

He sighed as my phone rang.

Without even saying hello, Hannah said, "Have you seen the paper? What's going on?"

"You mean with Mrs. Clatterbuck's weed-whacker?" I asked.

She clucked her tongue and said, "No! The skeleton! Even if the police don't know *who* the body is, surely it's news-worthy that there's a body at all!"

"I know. Something's fishy."

By Tuesday I'd expected to have reporters camped out on my lawn, scrambling for an interview. If it turned out that the body really was Stacy McFarland, Hannah and I would be heroes.

"I kind of hoped we'd get our pictures in the paper with Chaucer. They would interview us and then when school started kids would be like, 'Oh you're the girl from the newspaper!'"

"That's it! That's what we've got to do!" I said. "We need to send the photos to the press."

"But Officer Corker said not to tell anyone about the skeleton."

"True," I answered. "Let's call him and see if he knows anything yet."

"Can you come here?" Hannah asked. "My mom has a doctor's appointment, and I have to watch the brat."

Josey, a mini-Hannah with thick brown curls, answered the front door.

"Hey, Hank! Did you find any more dead bodies?"

So much for not telling anyone.

"Um, no," I answered as Hannah appeared at the top of the steps.

"He can't talk right now! We've got important business. Come on!" She motioned me up the stairs.

"I'm telling Mom you had a boy in your room!" Josey said contrarily.

"It's not a boy! It's Hank! So, go right ahead, you little rat-faced tattle-tale—have at it!"

Hannah yanked me into her room and slammed the door while I contemplated that, in her eyes, I wasn't a boy.

"Something major's going down!" She pointed to her computer. "I called Corker. His extension is on the police website."

"Okay?"

I looked around her room, which was now fully unpacked and decorated. From across the room, I noticed a photo of three curly-haired kids wearing Mickey Mouse ears. I stepped towards it to have a look, but Hannah pulled me over to her desk.

"Officer Corker wasn't available. Get this: *He's on vacation!* He left the day after you found the skull!" Hannah announced this in a way that let me know I should be aghast.

"Don't Pittsburgh cops go on vacation?"

Hannah shook her head at me. "Yes, cops in Pittsburgh go on vacation, but that's not the point. The point is that Officer Corker never mentioned *anything* to us about going on vacation. He talked like he'd be in town waiting anxiously for the medical examiner's report. He didn't say anything about going away. *And* it didn't sound like him on his voice mail."

"Let's call someone else," I suggested.

Hannah dialed the number for our friend, Marcia Masters, the keeper of records at the police department. She answered on the first ring.

"Hi, I'm trying to locate Officer Corker. I called his voicemail, and it said he's on vacation."

"Yes, that lucky dog!" she answered. "I've worked here for thirty-three years, and we've never had a vacation giveaway. Then *he* comes along and wins a free trip to Bollywood."

"Bollywood?" Hannah asked. "That amusement park with all the Indian rides?"

"It's a tribute to Hindi cinema," Officer Masters said indignantly, "and they produce more feature films each year than any other country in the world! Didn't you see *Ghetto Cat Billionaire*? It won all the awards last year."

I rolled my eyes into the phone. "When did Officer Corker leave?" Hannah asked.

"Sunday."

"Did he leave a forwarding phone number in case there's an emergency?"

"Chief Buckley's handling his cases while he's gone. Do you want me to transfer you?"

I nodded to Hannah and took the phone from her hand.

It rang twice before the chief answered with a twangy, "Buckley here."

"Chief Buckley, this is Hank Boyd."

"Who?"

"Hank Boyd, from Pelican Island. Last Saturday, I found a skeleton buried over there."

He answered with a moment of silence and then a click.

"He hung up on me!" I said. "Something major is going on! Who wins a trip that they have to leave for the next day?"

"I just can't believe that Officer Corker would leave town with such a big case—even if he *did* win a trip to Bollywood. I mean, jeez, it's Bollywood!"

"I know! The police department all the sudden starts giving away vacations to its employees and Officer Corker, who the chief basically ran off Pelican Island, is the first to win?"

AS SOON AS Hannah's mom got back from the doctor, we moved to my house.

"His first name was Steve, right?" Hannah asked as she thumbed through the meager Vista Point phone book.

"That's what his card says. But he said he's only lived here a few months, so I doubt he's in the phone book. Besides, who has landlines these days?"

Grandpa came in the kitchen and rummaged through the cabinets. "What're you kids up to today?"

"We're trying to figure out where Officer Corker lives," Hannah said.

"Who's that?"

I grunted. "The cop that came here last weekend after I found the skeleton on Pelican Island."

"Oh sure. He lives at the old Baxter place in Pine Acres, up on Gravely Street. Tom and Sara Baxter used to live there. It's the last house on the right, set back in the trees. They've been renting it out since they retired to Florida."

"How do you know that?" I asked.

"We were talking when y'all got back from the island. I don't know where you were." He looked at me. "Wait, I remember. You were with that friend of yours with the frizzy hair."

"Hannah?" I pointed at her with my thumb.

Grandpa examined Hannah's head of curls. "Yep, that's her."

She stuttered, "I—it's the humidity here."

Grandpa put his hand up to stop her. "No need to explain little lady. I'd try some argan oil or a keratin treatment. It could really help."

Grandpa watched a lot of infomercials.

He turned back to me. "That cop was telling me about how Buckley ran you off the island, and I was giving him the scoop on the chief and his family."

"What scoop?" I asked.

"How I built this house for your grandma right after I got back from Vietnam. The next year, Old Man Buckley started buying up all the land along the waterway from Moore's Landing down to Wilmington. That's how this neighborhood came about. Buckley couldn't get his hands on one two-acre plot of land right in the middle of where he wanted to develop, because the owner refused to sell. Buckley was angrier than a chicken in church!"

Hannah bounced in her seat with excitement. "It was here, wasn't it? *You* refused to sell to the Buckleys!"

Grandpa nodded. "After that, Old Man Buckley turned the bank on me. He got the president of the bank to call in the loan on the house."

"Did the Buckleys run the bank back then?" I asked.

"No, but it was the seventies. The economy was bad. I always suspected that Buckley offered McFarland that lot on the water if he agreed to call in my loan." Grandpa shook his head in disgust.

"McFarland?" I asked. "As in *Stacy* McFarland?"

"Her father, Michael. That's how he got that big house down at the other end of the street. They built it right after the bank came after us." Grandpa arched his eyebrows. "Coincidence? I don't think so!"

Hannah lifted her hands to motion around the kitchen. "So obviously, you got to keep your house."

"Yep. Elizabeth—that was my wife, God rest her soul—and I scraped together every cent we could. After McFarland got his lot down the street, he decided that what I had collected toward paying off the loan would be enough, even though it was only a thousand dollars."

"Do the Buckley's still own all the land around here?" Hannah asked.

"No. Bob Sr. bought it up, then sold it all off piece by piece to builders. He made millions," Grandpa answered. "There are three Buckley brothers, and the devil's got every single one of 'em on speed dial! Bob Jr. was a year ahead of me in high school, but we went to Vietnam around the same time. He got a cushy job translating communications between the Viet Cong. He didn't see any combat, but he got a head injury when he fell out of a chair over there. His father pulled some strings for him to get a medal for his noggin damage. It was a bunch of crap. He's had a tough time remembering things ever since—has to write everything down. I don't know how he got elected mayor, except for the fact that he's got straight teeth and a nice head of hair. When he came back from Nam, he got a job as a cop, based on his 'decorated' military service."

Grandpa scoffed and continued. "Chester's the middle brother and a blooming fool. That idiot couldn't decide what to wear without Bob telling him—and he wears a darn cop uniform to work." Grandpa shook his head.

"The youngest, Arthur, is the worst of all, a drunken slob. He worked for me as a bus driver back in the eighties. Somebody hired him when I was in the hospital with kidney stones. He hung out at a bar up on the highway, the Purple Pelican. The kids said they could smell liquor on his breath a lot. And he'd come into work looking like a gutter bum with cuts and bruises all over his face. Sometimes he'd just disappear for a week or two at a time. I tried to get rid of him for years. I'd call the police department and tell them that I suspected he was driving the bus drunk. Guess who they sent out to give him a sobriety test?" He shook his head. "Bob, his own brother!"

"I finally fired him for his excessive absences. Imagine if he had wrecked the bus. He could've killed somebody!"

25

Bollywood *is a theme park in western Tennessee owned by Indian film mogul Dhananhay Patel. An average of 2.5 million people visits each year. According to the International Association of Amusement Parks, approximately 1,500 people per year suffer a ride-related injury at an amusement park. For the story on amusement park deaths, see* Forensics 411 *episode 19, "Ticket to Die."*

YEARS OF KIDS riding their bikes had worn a shaded path between our neighborhood and Pine Acres. As we pedaled through the dark woods, enjoying the cooler temperatures the dense pine forest brought, I explained our location to Hannah. "Back that way is a place called 'The Compound.' It's where the high school jerks go to smoke, drink, and grope on the weekends. Don't go back there. Ever!"

"How come?" Hannah asked.

"Just don't," I answered. "Pine Acres is a bunch of old houses from back in the days when Vista Point had a mill. Most of them are rentals now." I pointed. "That's Gravely Street up ahead, where the path ends."

"Why are we going to Officer Corker's house if he's at Bollywood?"

"Just want to check something out."

We approached his house on the quiet, tree-lined street. I stopped to examine the decrepit gray box. A porch wrapped around the front and one side of the tiny, neglected house. The yard was a mixture of sand and pine needles, no grass.

"Is that it?" Hannah whispered.

"Why are you whispering?" I asked.

"It just seems like we should." She turned to me. "I don't see a car, and it doesn't look like anyone's home."

"Let's take a look."

As we inched toward the house, the porch light flashed on for just a second. "Did you see that?" I said.

"What?"

"The front light just flashed on and off." I tilted my head toward the house. "There it goes again."

We knocked on the door. A voice said, "Go around back."

Excitement coursed through my veins.

The rear porch was a four-foot square slab of cracked concrete. In a door with a torn screen stood Officer Corker. He opened the door and motioned for us to come in. "Well, well, it's the dynamic duo."

"You didn't go to Bollywood?" I asked.

"Um, no," he answered.

"There really was a free trip?" Hannah asked.

"Yes, but I think the fix was in for me to win. Officer Lubbock told me I'd won just as soon as I got back to the station from Pelican Island. There's never been a vacation giveaway before."

"Did you check the law enforcement missing persons databases?" I asked.

"That's the thing. When I got back to the station, I tried to log into the system. It allows me to search federal, state and county databases for crimes committed, missing persons, DMV records, arrest records, wanted criminals, et cetera."

"And?"

"The system was down. Lubbock was working on it but couldn't figure out what was wrong. The state maintains the database, and there was no problem at their end. Something was wrong with our local access."

"While she worked on it, I wanted to check out the McFarland file, but they'd already moved it to permanent storage." He explained, "They're renovating the records room and putting older files in off-site storage."

"Do you think the body might be Stacy McFarland?" Hannah asked excitedly. "Is that why you wanted to see her file?"

"I was mostly just curious," he answered. "So, I came home, but instead of packing for a week of fun and games on the Punjabi Python, I had my Mom and brother take my place. They were happy to get a free trip. I tried to get on the state database from my laptop here at home. I've done it plenty of times. But the system wouldn't take my username, so I called Lubbock. By then the system at the station was back up, but she couldn't log me in either. She said I wasn't showing up as an authorized user. That meant I couldn't get into *any* of the department's computers or databases. I'd logged on fine that morning."

"That seems weird," Hannah said.

"More like suspicious," I answered.

"The next day I drove my car to the airport in Wilmington and took a taxi back here. I've called Marcia several times to see if they could get me back in the system, but they can't. Some unknown 'administrator' removed me from everywhere. Marcia said not to worry about it and just enjoy my vacation. I've had my curtains drawn and lights out, trying to find out as much as I can about the McFarland case. Since Sunday, a patrol car's been driving past three times a day. It's like I'm under surveillance."

At that moment, Hannah and I looked at each other. We had to decide whether we were going to trust Officer Corker with the truth. Without words, and only a nod, we decided we would.

"So... um... we read the McFarland file," Hannah said.

"How?" Officer Corker asked.

"You don't want to know," I answered.

"You can get it out of storage, can't you?" Hannah asked Officer Corker.

"Not if I'm supposed to be at Bollywood."

"I thought you took pictures of the pages of the file?" I said.

"Oh, right, I totally forgot. They're on my tablet… at home."

"You took pictures of an official police file?" Corker asked.

"Basically," Hannah answered.

We waited for him to let us have it, but instead he said, "I'd like to check that out if you don't mind."

"Sure," Hannah answered.

I turned to Officer Corker. "There are some issues with the file and the investigation." I elaborated on the problems we'd found, including how it was a photocopy and the date on the report didn't mesh with when Bob Buckley said he found the journal.

"Based on my research," Corker said, "it seems to me that the Buckleys crossed paths with the McFarlands an awful lot. After talking to your grandfather, I checked on the county register of deeds, and there is no record of Michael McFarland *buying* the lot on Bending Oak Drive in 1975, just a transfer of the deed from Bob Buckley Sr. to McFarland. Then, of course, you told me how McFarland's daughter disappeared, and Bob Jr. was the investigating officer. Mix that with how the chief ran me off the island, how I was deleted from the police database system, and how I won a free trip to the Buckley's time-share, and I'm definitely curious."

"It was the *Buckley's* time-share at Bollywood?" Hannah asked.

Corker nodded. "Interesting, isn't it?"

"Have you called the morgue to find out the identity of the body?" I asked.

"Yes, but they won't release any information to me because they say I don't have proper authorization. Apparently, someone erased me from existence," Corker continued. "I figured I'd go straight to the county medical examiner. But, since our county is rural, without much of a tax base, and we don't have much violent crime, I found out we don't have a medical examiner."

"What about a coroner?" I asked. "I know a coroner's not a doctor, but do we at least have one of those?"

"Yes, but he's only part-time. The rest of the time he's the police chief," Corker answered.

"What?" Hannah threw her hands in the air. "This is insane! The district attorney needs to hear about this!"

Corker said, "I've called Chief Buckley thirteen times. He hasn't picked up. I keep leaving him messages, but he hasn't called me back yet. He may be avoiding me."

"Ya think?" Hannah asked.

"We still don't know whether the body from the island is Stacy McFarland or some other victim. It could be that the cops did a decent job investigating the McFarland disappearance and that the girl really did run away," Corker said.

Hannah argued, "But we know they botched the investigation because we found Michael McFarland's stolen bracelet in the woods next to my house."

"You did?" Corker asked.

It was time to show him all our cards. "If you thought the McFarland and Buckley paths crossed a lot before, wait 'til you hear this," I said.

I told him what I had learned from Doc Taylor about Stacy's journal and his scholarship to college. "Doc Taylor said he didn't know for sure that the journal was a fake. He thought *maybe* the cops had found it in an illegal search and then planted it in the locker so they could use it as evidence. But who knows."

"Either way, the journal is a questionable piece of evidence that conveniently disappeared," Hannah said.

"And why would Chief Buckley not return your calls?" I asked. "There's something about that skeleton that he doesn't want anyone to know."

"It could be that it's Stacy McFarland and Chief Buckley is trying to protect Bob Jr. You know, so people don't find out that Mayor Buckley didn't *really* solve the case when he was a cop."

"But why?" Corker asked. "*If* the journal was a fake, why make it?"

"So, Mayor Buckley could say he solved the case back then," Hannah answered. "He'd be a hero."

"But not if the body showed up after all these years," I said. "That would make Bob look like a fool, a liar, or both."

"That's a lot of illegal maneuvering just to close a case," Corker countered.

"Why don't you come back to my house and have a look at the investigation file? You can stay there if you want so you can move more freely."

"That sounds tempting. I'm about to run out of frozen dinners."

After Corker left the room, Hannah hissed, "Why is the file at your house? You told me you returned it."

I swallowed hard. "Um, I did take it back to the station."

She put her hands on her hips. "But you just invited the cop back to your house to look at the file. What's that about?"

Heat traveled up my neck.

She stared at me with those eyes and tapped her toe impatiently on the floor.

"I—I meant... I meant that you could get your tablet and bring it up to my house and then Corker could look at the pictures of the file."

My stammer gave me away.

"You're lying!" Hannah said.

"Not really," I mumbled. "I said I took it back to the station. Which I did."

"But you didn't *put* it back?" She got her hackles up. "Why not?"

"I ran into a little trouble."

Her eyes narrowed. "What kind of trouble?"

"It doesn't matter. Okay? I still have the file. Let's just go back to my house and let Corker look at it."

"Does it have something to do with why your nose was all swollen?"

"Can you just drop it?" I snapped.

"Fine. Whatever," she grumbled. "I thought we were friends. But friends don't lie to each other or keep secrets." She pushed past me.

THAT DAY ENDED with another text from Dillon: You think 6th grade was bad - wait til next year!

I sat on the floor against the bed and buried my head in my hands. I wanted to respond, "Bring it on jack-wagon," but instead I kicked myself for breaking Dr. Blanchard's number one rule for Dillon the Villain: Do Not Engage. I pounded my feet on the carpet. "Crap, crap, crap!" So much for my fresh start in high school.

26

When searching a crime scene for trace evidence, investigators usually search in a geometric pattern. The most common are the grid, a shoulder to shoulder linear search, dividing the search area into quadrants or searching in a spiral outward from a key piece of evidence, such as a body. See Forensics 411 episode 16, "The Truth Is Out There."

THE NEXT MORNING, Officer Corker was still sleeping in my room when I heard my mom in the kitchen making coffee.

"Oh hey, Sweetie. Did you sleep okay on the couch?"

"Yeah. Thanks for letting Officer Corker stay."

Mom snorted. "When you asked if a friend could spend the night, I assumed it would be someone under the age of thirty."

"Have I ever had a friend spend the night?"

Her shoulders slumped. "Well no, but there's a first time for everything."

I patted her on the back. "Chin up Mom, someday I'll make an actual friend."

Mom looked me in the eye and said, "I think you already

have." She cocked her head toward my bedroom. "And I'm not talking about the man sleeping in there."

"You mean Hannah?" I asked, playing it cool.

"Yes. Grandpa says you two spend every day together."

I shrugged. "We're working the McFarland case. She's, you know... smart."

Mom took a deep breath. "I'm glad to see you putting yourself out there. Hannah seems like a nice girl."

"Yeah, she's pretty cool. Just don't make a big deal out of it, okay?"

"Fine," Mom said. "What's on your agenda today?"

"Hannah's dad's a lawyer and was supposed to talk to the district attorney last night. We're hoping he got a report from Chief Buckley or the CSI team that processed the skeleton. Then we're going to search the wooded area south of Hannah's house to see if we can find any more clues that the cops missed back in 1985."

"So, just a typical day, huh?" Mom smiled as she zipped up her purse. "Gotta go to work."

"Thanks for being so understanding about Officer Corker. You're a really good mom."

She spun back around and said, "Thanks, Sweetie. That means a lot."

Just as the door closed behind Mom, Steve came out of my room.

I held up the newspaper. "Nothing in the news *again*."

"That doesn't surprise me," he said. "I had an epiphany last night. I realized that the remains should've gone to the crime lab in Jacksonville, not the county morgue. I just called there and told the clerk that I wanted the state medical examiner's results from the skeletal remains that were recovered from Pelican Island on Saturday."

"And?"

"He said, 'What remains?'"

I threw the newspaper down. "What? How is that even possible?"

At that moment, my phone rang.

Hannah said, "This is a purely professional call about the case. I'm *still* not talking to you."

I hadn't realized that she wasn't talking to me. But now that she mentioned it, she hadn't said much after our exchange about the file.

"Okay." I kept it business-like as well. "Do you have any new information?" I put her on speaker.

"Dad called Mark Ellis last night. Then Mr. Ellis called the SBI field office in Jacksonville. Apparently, that's where the body should've been sent since our county doesn't have a medical examiner."

"And let me guess," I interrupted. "Buckley didn't submit a body to them."

"Exactly!"

"Did Mark Ellis say whether he could do anything?" I asked.

"He could request the coroner's records of the body found on Pelican Island *if* there were any. But apparently, Chief Buckley didn't document finding the body. In fact, Mr. Ellis checked, and officially, there's no record of Officer Corker being called to your house last weekend!"

"What?" Corker said.

"But wait, it gets even better! When my dad said something to Mark Ellis about the CSI team, Mr. Ellis said that Vista Point doesn't have a CSI team!" Hannah scoffed. "Can you believe that?"

"Then, who were the two guys that showed up with Chief Buckley?" I asked.

Steve ran his hands through his hair and paced the kitchen. "I can't believe this! How can they just bury this whole thing?"

"Tell Steve I heard what he said and no, they can't!" Hannah said. "We still have the photos. I think it's time that we take our case to the press!"

"You're right! Chief Buckley doesn't know we have photos of the skull!" I said. "We need to send them to the papers and the news stations—"

"No," Steve said, "we need to send them to Brian."

"Who's Brian?" I asked.

"Brian Watts. He's a buddy of mine that works for the State Bureau of Investigation. He might be able to help us."

"Thanks for the info," I said to Hannah. "I'll talk to you later."

"No, you won't, because we're still not speaking!" She hung up.

"Look," Steve explained, "we don't want to send that photo to the paper. It'll tip off whoever has the skeleton that we're on to them. We need to go back to Pelican Island and see if the body is there. Maybe they just buried it back. It's important for us to find out *where* that body is if it's not at the morgue or the SBI crime lab. If there's no skeleton, there's no proof that someone died."

"But I have the photos."

"Sure, but we haven't ID'd the skeleton, and we don't have proof of where you found it. I fear that Chief Buckley is going to say there is *no* body and that you and Hannah are just a couple of attention-seeking kids. They can say you staged that photo with a fake skull. Since I'm at Bollywood, I can't tell the press anything different. They can say Hannah's dad was just fooled by your fake skull."

"I think the chief is willing to do just about anything to keep that skeleton a secret," I said. "There's got to be something important about it."

I called Hannah and explained our plans. "We're going to go back to the island to see if the skeleton is still there. I need you to go back to the woods where we found the nugget bracelet and search for more clues. Don't worry about going fast, just be thorough. Search for things that look like they might've been there since 1985."

"What's the magic word?"

"Please?" I answered. "Oh, and um, if you have time, you should watch *Forensics 411* Episode 16. It explains how to search a crime scene properly."

"I'll get right on that," she said and hung up.

27

A rson is the criminal act of setting fire to a property. Frequently, arson is committed to cover up another crime such as murder. Most arsonists don't realize that a fire must reach a temperature of 2,700 degrees Fahrenheit to obliterate bones. See Forensics 411 episode 15, "Fired Up."

I LOADED SHOVELS, trash bags and a cooler full of ice and waters onto *Crime Cat*. When I got back, Steve was standing in the kitchen with Chaucer and his leash.

"What are you doing?" I asked.

"I think we should take him to the island with us. He found the skeleton one time. He might find it again if it's there."

"No."

"That's not a bad idea," Grandpa said. "He's all healed up, isn't he?"

"He's better, but I don't want to risk losing him again."

"We could keep him on a leash," Steve suggested.

"You weren't there. Chaucer nearly died the last time he went to Pelican Island. I won't let that happen again!"

"I grew up with hunting dogs," Steve said as if this made

him an expert on animals.

"Well, Chaucer's not a hunter."

"He really isn't," Grandpa said. "Believe me, I tried."

"He almost died on that island because he couldn't say no to his nose. I won't put him through that again."

"Boomer," Grandpa said.

"It's Hank, Grandpa."

"Whatever!" He waved his hand at me. "You know I've never thought that dog could catch a cold in a kindergarten class, but he definitely proved that he's got some real searching instinct. If you don't take him back there, you're denying him what he was born to do. It might be that search and rescue is that dog's calling."

Grandpa had never complimented Chaucer's abilities as a hound dog.

I approached Chaucer, bent down, and whispered in his ear, "You don't want to go back there, do you?" In any court of law it would be considered a leading question.

My barely-healed dog barked, stood up and wagged his tail enthusiastically.

"That looks like a yes to me," Grandpa said.

Against my better judgment, I agreed.

AT THE DOCK, Chaucer turned circles impatiently as I tried to start the boat. It didn't cooperate. As Steve was coming down the dock from the house, I found the issue and showed it to him.

"Are you kidding me? Someone actually cut your fuel line? This is unreal! We're being sabotaged."

"They sliced it long-ways, so I didn't notice it until I tried to start her up." It was a smart move.

I got out of the boat. "Someone doesn't want you to have access to any police records and doesn't want me to get back to that island!"

"Does Hannah have a boat?"

"No." I looked at *Crime Cat*. "But I can get a new fuel line at the hardware store up on the highway."

"Does your grandfather have a car?" Steve asked.

"No, we had to sell it when he went on a bit of a rampage in the Stop-n-Shop parking lot. Some kid took the parking place he wanted, so Grandpa rammed his car out of the spot. They caught it all on security cameras."

"Man, he's a pistol," the officer said.

"It's the dementia. He didn't use to be so ornery," I answered.

"I can ride my bike to the hardware store. It's only a few miles."

Steve reached in his pocket. "Here's money for the fuel line and get a cheap set of walkie-talkies if they have them."

THE CUT FUEL line set us back about two hours. By the early afternoon, we arrived at Pelican Island and beached the boat on the marsh side, opposite the Devil's Backbone.

Pointing with his front paw in the direction of the large dunes in the center of the island, Chaucer let out a tortured howl, followed by a series of whimpers and yelps. I couldn't reason with him. As soon as I untied him from the boat, he took off in a gallop, ripping the leash from my hands.

He headed toward the Devil's Backbone but kept me informed of his location with howls and barks. I ran behind him, trying to keep up with his four powerful legs.

As we drew closer to the dune, Chaucer released a blood-curdling sound. "I'm coming, boy!"

"Right behind you!" Steve yelled.

Minutes passed without any sounds, and I panicked, fearing the worst.

Finally, I arrived at the set of dunes where I thought the skeleton had been.

The police tape was gone. The hole was gone.

I bent over to catch my breath.

At the top of the highest dune, I called Chaucer's name. He didn't answer.

Finally, I heard another anguished howl and turned toward the sound.

"I hear ya boy! Keep talking! I'm coming!"

His barking came from an area southeast of the dunes. With the walkie-talkie, I sent Steve in that direction and repeatedly called Chaucer as I ran toward his howls.

I spotted him about fifty yards away, lying in the sand, whining. With him in sight, I down-shifted to a jog to slow my pounding heart.

"What is it, boy? What did you find?" He looked up at me, beside himself with grief, and let out a pain-filled yelp. He turned his head to gaze at the remains of a campfire.

I bent down, still trying to catch my breath, and rubbed his head. "It's okay."

I circled the campfire, examining it from every angle. In the ashes, a shard of bone caught my eye.

"In fact, you did great!" I rubbed his ears. "I see what you found. You're such a good search dog!"

Through static, Steve spoke. "Hank, I have a visual of you. Is everything all right?"

"I think we're a little too late," I said.

Chaucer howled.

Steve came up behind me, lugging the shovels, trash bags, and a cooler, gasping. "What do we have?"

I pointed to the campfire.

Steve put on a pair of latex gloves and began sifting through the ashes and debris of the fire.

He saw the bone, and what looked like part of a second one. I leaned closer while trying to console Chaucer with my other hand.

"I'm pretty sure it's a radius bone," I said. "That's part of the forearm. Not sure about the other one. Looks like maybe part of a femur."

"Let's bag them," Steve said, opening the plastic bag. "As a police officer, I'm embarrassed to ask you this, but can you get DNA from ashes?"

"No. But since the bones are not completely burned, a forensic biologist might be able to cut the bone, grind it to a powder then mix it with a special enzyme. After that, he could separate the DNA from the rest of the cell material, *if* he has the right equipment."

Steve stopped me. "So, the answer is *no*?"

"The answer is maybe. DNA degrades over time, so there's no telling."

"Great," Steve answered. "Then there's still hope to at least find out who this used to be."

After an hour of sifting through the ashes, we found what we suspected were a few more pieces of bone then set out for the dunes where Chaucer initially found the skeleton. It took all my strength to drag him away from the fire site. It wasn't until Steve let him sniff the bag with the bones in it, that he agreed to go with us.

Once we got close to the dunes, Chaucer ripped the leash from my hands and took off again. He stopped when he reached the location of his former hole and let out a stratosphere-piercing howl.

He dug furiously.

I tried to pull him away. "No, you can't! Your paws are barely healed. You have to stop!" I looked to Steve for help.

Steve yanked on Chaucer's collar as hard as he could to help me get control of him.

"Take him!" Steve ordered as he handed me the leash. "Take him back to the boat and wait there. He thinks something's here, and he hasn't been wrong yet."

28

R obbery and burglary both involve property theft. If people are in the home when the theft occurs and threatened with force, the theft is a "robbery." If no one is in the property when the theft occurs, it is a "burglary." The state with the highest robbery rate per person is Mississippi. The state with the lowest per capita robbery rate is New York. See Forensics 411 episode 12, "Crossing the Line."

I USED the time at the boat to explore an aspect of the McFarland case that I foolishly hadn't considered. I chalked it up to my bathing suit-induced lobotomy.

Using my phone, I opened the "Local Real Estate" folder that I'd begun during the housing crisis. Yes, I was once a first grader with a penchant for not only the boomerang, but, stocks, bonds and real estate. At six I understood what "too big to fail" meant, but couldn't tie my own shoes.

I clicked the link for the McFarland house listing and scrolled through the pictures from when it was for sale. First, I looked at the garage just to make sure that it was on the south side of the house as I remembered. Hannah's parents had moved the garage to the north side during renovations.

Next, I enlarged the photos of the front and scrolled to pictures of other exterior doors. They had deadbolt locks on all of them.

I rubbed Chaucer's ears. "The news articles said all the McFarland's doors and windows were locked when they got home, and that Stacy's keys were on the kitchen counter. How could Stacy run away and lock the deadbolts behind her if her keys were still inside the house? That's not possible."

I scrolled through each photo looking for the room that opened into the garage. It was a long narrow laundry room with a doorway at both ends. The first one was where the photographer had stood to take the picture. The second door went into the garage. I zoomed in, making the door as large as I could, and then I knew.

"Yes!" The door from the laundry room into the garage didn't have a deadbolt lock on it.

I looked at Chaucer. "You know what I need to check next, don't you?"

He didn't seem to have a clue.

I read the room by room details of the house.

"And there it is! That's how the burglar got in the house!"

Chaucer sat up and alerted me that Steve was on his way back.

"I found a piece of fabric," he called as he was approaching. "Seems like it might be what we saw underneath the skeleton last time. It feels like canvas. I'll have the SBI test it along with the partial bones we found."

"And I figured out how the McFarland's burglar got in the house with all the doors and windows locked."

"How?" Steve asked.

"An automatic garage door opener," I explained. "According to the police report, Mr. McFarland's car was unlocked in the driveway. I checked the specs on the McFarland house, and it had an automatic garage door. That was high-tech for a house built in the seventies. Unlike the rest of the doors, the entry from the garage into the home did not have a deadbolt. If Mr. McFarland left his car unlocked, the burglar could've used the automatic garage door opener to get in the house. I bet the burglar was in the garage and that's how the McFarland's lawn chair ended up on the floor."

Steve nodded. "That's right! I remember reading about the chair in the report."

Chaucer faced toward the dunes and wailed one last time for the soul buried on Pelican Island.

29

O scar Wilde once said, *"The truth is rarely pure and never simple."* For more information about truth, lies, polygraphs, and the interrogation process, see Forensics 411 *episode 20, "Those Lying Eyes."*

I CALLED Hannah when we returned to my house in the early evening to see about her progress in the woods.

She answered with, "Have you decided to tell me what happened at the police station?"

I bit the proverbial bullet and told her the truth-ish. "I... um... I got ambushed."

"Where?"

"At the police station."

"By whom?" She knew when to use *whom* and loved to flaunt it.

"I'm not sure. I was getting ready to unlock the storage unit when someone grabbed me from behind and knocked me to the ground. He was huge. I tried to fight him off, but he was so much bigger than me. He tried to steal my backpack. I fought him for it, but he stole some money I had in it." This, of course, was a lie. Every cent I owned was in my closet shoe box.

"Oh, my gosh, I'm so sorry," Hannah said with a sympathetic tone. "Did you report it to the police?"

"Consider what you just asked me."

"Oh right," she agreed. "Does your mom know?"

"No. She thinks I hurt my nose on the island, and we need to keep it that way."

"Okay," she answered. "I'm sorry that happened to you."

Did that mean she forgave me?

"Thanks," I answered. "How was your search of the woods?"

"I found a few things of interest."

"Can you bring what you found to my house?"

"Sure. I'll tell my parents you invited me for dinner."

"Wait—don't hang up. I figured out how the robber got in the McFarland's house."

After explaining my revelation, Hannah said, "Well, duh! Why didn't we think of that before?"

"Who knows?" I answered.

"Hey, I found something else too," Hannah said. "It's a sticky note with some weird words on it. It was under the table in our basement. It smells like it came out of the McFarland file."

"You sniffed it?" I asked. "Why'd you do that?"

"To see what it smells like!"

And people thought I was weird.

"Well, by all means, bring the mephitic sticky note with you, too," I instructed.

"Ooh, *mephitic*, that's a nice one!" Hannah said.

30

D NA exists in nearly every tissue and fluid in the human body. Saliva has no cells, but epithelial cells collect in the salivary glands, which have DNA. See Forensics 411 episode 7, "The Secrets of the Body."

AFTER GOBBLING FROZEN PIZZAS, Steve, Hannah, Grandpa, and I donned latex gloves and sifted through the bags of stuff Hannah had collected in the woods. I was lucky to have a mom and grandfather who supported my interests.

Mom took the job of recording each item in a notebook. Hannah was supposed to have gathered up any items that looked like they had been in the woods since 1985. Beyond that, we didn't really know what we were looking for.

Grandpa spoke first. "Well, this thing is old." He held up a soda bottle and shoved it toward me. "They stopped making this crap a long time ago."

"New Coke?" I read the faded label on the glass bottle. For real, a glass soda bottle.

Mom said, "I learned about that in college. It was one of the worst marketing disasters in history. The Coca-Cola Company was tired of being second to Pepsi, so they came up with a new formula for Coke that was meant to attract Pepsi drinkers. They called it *New Coke*. Loyal Coke drinkers hated the new formula. People started hoarding the old Coke and wrote hate letters to Coca-Cola. It only took a few months for Coca-Cola to realize that they had made a colossal mistake. They yanked it from stores and remarketed the original Coke formula under the name *Coca-Cola Classic*."

Steve looked up from his phone. "That was in 1985! Coca-Cola first released the new version of Coke on April 23rd and stopped selling it in most places three months later!" He picked up the Coke bottle that Grandpa had set down. "That means this New Coke is probably from the time that Stacy McFarland disappeared! We'll send it to the SBI to test for fingerprints and DNA. My friend Brian is going to try to fast-track our stuff through the forensic lab."

Hannah had to leave at ten. As soon as she left, I got a text from her: 4got 2 show u the sticky note.

Around midnight my mom said, "Gentlemen, I have to go to sleep. Not all of us get a week-long vacation to Bollywood." She winked at Steve.

"Thanks for all your help, Angela. I really appreciate it," Officer Corker said.

"No problem. Let me know if you need me to give you a ride to your car in the morning."

"Thanks, but I don't want to be a bother."

"Oh, it's no problem. I'm happy to help." She tilted her head to the side and smiled just like Hannah does.

"How about if I take you out to breakfast to thank you for your help and hospitality?" Steve suggested.

I looked at Mom.

"That'd be nice." She ran a hand through her red hair.

I looked to Steve.

"We'll call it a date." He smiled and nodded.

Then I looked at Mom. It was like watching a tennis match.

"Um, sure." Mom blushed as she turned toward her bedroom.

Steve and Angela? When did they get on a first name basis? Breakfast? A date? My mom didn't date.

After she left the kitchen, I narrowed my gaze at Steve.

He patted my hand and said, "It's just a meal. Your mom's been really nice to help us."

31

Forty-nine of the 50 states in the U.S. have a statewide police agency with authority to conduct law enforcement and criminal investigations outside the authority of the sheriff. They can also coordinate multi-jurisdictional task forces in serious or complicated cases. See Forensics 411 *episode 14, "Who's in Charge?"*

OFFICER CORKER RETURNED from his breakfast date around 9:30.

"You were up and out of here early this morning," I said.

"I couldn't sleep after we finished going through the stuff Hannah found."

"Are we pretending that you didn't just get back from a date with my mom?"

"We just went to breakfast. She's been kind enough to let me stay here and helped us sort through all the stuff last night. I just wanted to thank her for everything."

"Are you saying she's not good enough to take out on a *real* date?" I asked.

"Um… no." Steve looked at me. "I'm sorry, but I'm confused. Are you mad at me because I took your mom out on a date, or because *I didn't?*"

"Both!" I snarled.

"Neither!" I shook my head.

"I don't know." I turned away, feeling embarrassed that I had brought it up.

"Look, don't make this out to be more than it is. I took your mom out to breakfast to thank her for letting me stay here. That's it. I'm not trying to take the place of your father or anything."

"Don't talk about my father!" I yelled. "You don't know anything about him!"

He put his hands in the air as if to surrender. "Fine. I'm sorry."

I looked him in the eyes and said, "Just so you know, I have a certain set of boomeranging skills that could make me a nightmare for a person like you."

"I'll definitely take that under consideration." Steve chuckled as if I were joking. "Can I give you an update on the case?"

"Yes," I grunted.

"I talked with my friend Brian Watts at the SBI first thing this morning. He shared my email with his supervisor, Special Agent Horton. Brian says that his supervisor is interested in what's going on here: the missing skeleton, the lack of a police report, my deleted existence as a cop. They are going to check things out from the angle that Chester Buckley may have obstructed justice by destroying the skeleton. He's the one with the means and opportunity to do it."

"Good."

"Brian wants me to take the Coke bottle, bones, and fabric we found to the lab in Jacksonville for testing. His boss got us moved to the top of the list. We need to be there in an hour. I know you live for this forensics stuff, so I'm guessing you'd like to come along."

"Definitely!"

"I figured. Will Hannah want to come?"

"I'll call her."

Hannah didn't answer the phone, so I texted her with our plans.

She texted back when we were on our way to the SBI lab: `Can't make it. Have an appointment. Here's pix of the sticky note from the basement.` It said:

THUC DIEU TRONG NHOT NHAT CON GAI

32

Investigators can use DNA to solve crimes. If police have a suspect in mind, they can take a sample of that person's DNA and compare it to evidence from the crime scene. The results of this comparison may help prove whether the suspect committed the crime. In cases without a suspect, investigators analyze and compare biological evidence from the crime scene to offender profiles in DNA databases. When this is successful, it is called a "cold hit." Since the early 1990s, most states require convicted felons to submit samples of their DNA to these databases. See Forensics 411 episode 7, "Secrets of the Body."

THE FORENSIC SPECIALIST'S assistant at the SBI took our evidence in as soon as we arrived and arranged a tour of the facility. It was exciting to see them do all the things I hoped to do someday.

Around noon, Agent Watts arrived from Raleigh with his boss, Patrick Horton, and they took Corker and me to lunch. Both agents were unnaturally beefy, meticulously dressed, very intimidating African-American men in their 40s.

"It's interesting," Agent Horton said, taking a notepad out of the pocket of his navy-blue suit. "I checked our records to see if we helped the Vista Point police with the McFarland case back in 1985. Under most circumstances, the SBI only steps into an investigation if the local authorities ask for our help. They didn't. Brian researched all the media accounts of the investigation, and it sounds like the investigating officer, Bob Buckley, had no leads whatsoever. That's just the kind of case where locals usually call in the SBI."

Agent Watts added, "We don't have authority to investigate the McFarland case itself. It was closed back in '85. The best I can do, *officially*, is investigate the skeleton you found on Pelican Island. I'll try to find out why Buckley didn't send it to the state crime lab, and why there's no record of Hank's call to the police. Then we'll see what the lab turns up on the items you brought in this morning. We'll try to connect some dots."

After lunch, the agents headed to the police station in Vista Point to speak with Chief Buckley. We returned to the SBI office as the technicians were finishing their first examinations of the New Coke bottle and the piece of fabric that Steve had found in Chaucer's hole.

JULIA, the lab technician, led us from the waiting room into an office and motioned for us to sit. "I have good news and bad news. The bad news is that there are no readable fingerprints on any of these things. That's not surprising. Like you suspected, these items are decades old, and they've been outdoors for years."

I nodded to disguise my disappointment.

"However, the Coke bottle is a DNA gold mine. It seems that someone spit in it then sealed the lid, preserving their DNA for posterity. If there's enough DNA to create a profile, we can run it through CODIS."

"Great!" I said. CODIS was the Combined DNA Index

System compiled by the FBI. It allowed federal, state and local crime labs to access and compare DNA profiles electronically.

"Yes. However, law enforcement agencies didn't start taking DNA samples from suspects until the early 1990s. It's possible that the person who spit in the bottle has no police record. Or, they had an arrest *before* the early nineties. In which case, the saliva residue in the bottle won't be of any help."

"Unless we can come up with a suspect to get a DNA sample from," I said.

"Yes, but based on what you've said, it doesn't sound like there were any known suspects at the time of the crime, right?" the technician countered.

"What about the bone and fabric?" Officer Corker asked.

"Our forensic pathologist is examining them and running tests, but he won't know anything until next week. Extracting the DNA from the fabric and the bones, if there is any, running the samples, and analyzing the data takes time. However, if you want to hang around a few hours more, we should at least have some preliminary information to tell you if we've got a large enough DNA sample to create a profile."

"Oh, we're waiting!" I answered, without even checking with Corker.

While he went to the vending machine, I texted Hannah to see if she'd learned anything about the smelly sticky note.

She texted back: `Been working all day. Think writing is Vietnamese. It might translate into: It is in the most crowded.`

I texted back: `What does that mean?`

Hannah responded: `Patience, child. Patience!`

TWO HOURS later Julia returned with a folder. "We've got a small, but useable DNA sample from the bones and fabric. It appears there were some tiny blood droplets on the fabric. We should have some answers for you around Wednesday."

"Wednesday?" I argued. "But we can't wait until then. Somebody already destroyed the skeleton, removed the record of Steve's visit to my house, and tampered with my boat. Who knows what else they can do between now and Wednesday?"

"Sorry, the pathologist doesn't work on weekends. These things take time."

33

*I*f *a tracking device is installed on your phone, you may receive unusual text messages or see a distorted phone screen. Your phone may shut down uncontrollably or have a shorter battery life than normal. Likewise, your phone may seem physically warmer than usual. This software is the modern version of phone tapping. See* Forensics 411 *episode 25, "Control, Alt, Delete."*

R U AWAKE? I texted Hannah at nine the next the morning.

`No. I'm asleep.`

`Can I come over? We've got some work to do.`

`Come @ 10.`

That gave me time to private message `Hacktivist77` through my *Forensics 411* page.

`Need ur help again.`

In less than five minutes he sent me an encrypted link for us to communicate.

`What do you need?`

`Can you set up a tap on a cell phone?`

`It'll cost you.`

Of course. `How much?`

$100.

That wasn't bad.

Per day. I take all major credit cards and select cryptocurrencies.

You realize I'm only fourteen, right?

He typed, Sorry, need to make a living. Got kids.

I pictured Hacktivist77 at the park pushing his kids on the swings, wearing a ski mask to conceal his identity.

I opened the shoe box that held my emergency cash. I had counted 247 dollars and some change the last time I'd contacted Hacktivist77. That was enough for almost two-and-a-half days of phone taps on Chief Buckley's cell phone. I typed: Will I be able to monitor all his calls - incoming and outgoing?

Of course. But you can't use a cell phone to monitor the tap because it's too easy for cell carriers at both ends to trace a third-party tap. Use a computer, iPad, or tablet. I'll need the IP address of the device you're going to use. Do you have that?

I figured it was best to use Hannah's tablet because ours was a desktop computer in the den. I typed: I'll have to get it.

Hacktivist77 responded: As soon as you can, text the IP address. I can't do much without it. After your payment clears and you've given me the address, I'll get to work on the tap. I'll send you a link with directions. Download it to the computer as soon as you get it, then delete the link from your phone. I'll be sending it from a dummy IP address that will only stay live for ten minutes. Do you want to prepay for a certain number of days or pay day-to-day?

`Day-to-day for now,` I answered. `It's all I can afford.` I tried to sound pitiful.

`Who do you want me to tap?`

I gave him the phone number.

`Who's the number belong to?`

I texted: `Chester Buckley - the Vista Point police chief.`

`In that case, it's only $50 bucks a day. Taps on the fuzz are 50% off. It's my blue-light special.` He added an uncharacteristic smiley face at the end.

`How long until you have the tap set up?`

`Two hours after I get payment. Remember, if you get busted, you never heard of me.`

`Got it,` I answered, feeling a keen sense of excitement. I'd never tapped someone's phone before.

`I mean it, kid. If you roll over on me, I can easily access your school records, your parents' bank accounts, change the name or amount on the mortgage - anything.`

`You can trust me,` I typed.

The link through which we were communicating disappeared.

At 10:05 I rang Hannah's doorbell.

"Hi, Hank," Mrs. Simmons said as she opened the door. "How's your dog?"

"Fine, thank you."

"Hannah's upstairs."

She was waiting at the top of the steps.

"Do you have your tablet up here?" I asked as I closed the door behind me.

Hannah blushed. "Um, my mom says we have to keep the door open since you're... like... a boy."

"Oh," I answered. *It's about time someone recognized I was a guy!*

She re-opened the door.

I lowered my voice. "I've arranged for a tap on Chief Buckley's cell phone."

"`Hacktivist77`?"

"Yeah, but it's gonna cost fifty dollars a day."

"You're kidding!"

"I know. It's expensive, but that's his 'blue-light special' for law enforcement taps. If we were tapping a regular citizen, it would cost twice as much."

34
──────

The Vietnamese writing system differs from other major eastern languages such as Japanese, Chinese, and Korean because, like English, it uses the Latin alphabet. If you're looking for a career in forensics but don't like dead bodies, you can become a forensic linguist. See Forensics 411 *episode 18, "Forensics for the Living."*

WE PAID `Hacktivist77` with a pre-paid debit card I bought at a gas station on Fripp Road. While he set up the tap, Hannah and I tackled the sticky note.

She took it out of her desk and shoved it in my face. "Here. Sniff it! It smells like the files from the police station."

"Are you like a human-bloodhound hybrid?" I asked, not wanting to sniff her sticky note.

Looking smug, she said, "My olfactory system runs at a higher throttle than most. It's a gift and a curse."

"Is that how you sniff out love triangles?"

"Touché," she answered, and wouldn't take it away from my face until I pretended to take a big whiff of sticky note.

"I've been working on some things. Like I texted you, I think it's Vietnamese. The entire phrase means 'it is in the most crowded.' But when I type each word into Google translate individually rather than as a phrase it means "real god in viscous best with" and *gai* doesn't translate into English."

"Have you tried rearranging the words in a different order. Not all languages have the same syntax as English," I said.

"Yes," she chuckled, "the meanings get even weirder."

"What about pairing words to see if they make a word or phrase that makes sense? Like instead of typing in just *thuc* try *thuc dieu*."

"Yep. *Thuc dieu* together means 'termination of.' *Dieu trong* means 'so important.' *Trong nhot nhat* translates into 'looks pale.'"

We continued pairing words together. "Google Translate wants me to add accents or carets or some other weird symbols above or below the letters to get a translation." Hannah curled her lip. "The sticky note doesn't have any symbols other than letters. That's a huge problem. There are a lot of different versions of letters in the Vietnamese alphabet. An *a* with an accent is different from an *a* with a caret on top. Then there's an *a* with a dot underneath it. Each one is a different letter. It's insane."

I took out my phone. "I'll check out other translating sites."

We typed away on our devices for the time it took `Hacktivist77` to get the wiretap set up and message me that it should be ready on Hannah's tablet. He'd done it all remotely, which was both cool and scary.

"Are you sure it's even Vietnamese?"

"I'm ninety-seven percent positive. The letter combinations don't seem to be a romance or Germanic language. There are only a few Asian languages that use our alphabet, and Vietnamese is one of them. Besides, your grandfather told us Mayor Buckley worked as a translator during the Vietnam war."

I snapped my fingers. "You're brilliant!"

"I know," she answered without looking up.

After a few minutes she said, "Bingo!" and bounced on her bed.

"What'd you find?"

"When I add some accents and squiggles to some of the letters, I get a different translation: The real thing is in pale daughter."

"*Trong* only translates into 'in' as far as I can figure," she said, furiously working her keyboard. "It seems like this is talking about something being 'in' something else. And *nhot* also translates into 'slimy,' not just 'viscous.'"

"Okay, you keep working on that. Since you need your tablet for that, are you willing to take the first overnight shift of monitoring Chief Buckley's calls?"

"Sure," she answered. "What do I have to do?"

"Just keep the computer on and plugged in with the volume turned up loud enough to wake you. If Chief Buckley makes or receives a call, you will get an audible alert, like a beep or buzz. Then you click on that icon." I pointed to her screen. "According to `Hacktivist77` your tablet should automatically record the call."

"Got it," she said. "Can you see yourself out? I want to keep working on these translations while I'm in the zone."

"Sure," I answered.

"See you tomorrow," she said.

I knew that she meant it.

35

In many states, it takes more hours of training to become a licensed barber, interior designer, or refrigeration technician than it takes to become a police officer. The most substantial amount of time goes into training officers with fire-arm skills and emergency medical services. Trainees spend approximately twelve hours learning about physical evidence. See Forensics 411 episode 2, "The Basics."

I WOKE on the couch to the sound of laughter in the kitchen. Steve and my mom were sitting at the kitchen table drinking coffee. Mom was in her pajamas. (*Her pajamas!*)

"Morning, Sweetie," Mom said in a chipper voice. "Did you sleep well?"

"Until your cackling woke me up!"

She didn't respond with words, but the shape of her mouth communicated that she didn't like my tone.

"Um, I didn't mean that. I just…"

She gave me the look that meant I was supposed to apologize.

I mumbled, "Sorry."

She smiled, then motioned for me to come sit next to her.

"Steve was telling me that you're getting closer to an answer on whether that skeleton is Stacy McFarland."

"What time is it?" I asked. "Why haven't you left for work?"

"It's Saturday."

"Oh, right."

Steve added, "Yes, I'm supposed to be back from Bollywood on Monday night."

"Then you'll be sleeping at your own house, right?" I glared and shot all sorts of non-verbal communications at him.

"Boomer, you're being rude to our guest," Mom said. "Apologize."

Since when was Officer Corker "our" guest?

"Call me Hank!" I snapped.

"Apologize," Mom said with more insistence.

I hated apologies. Seriously, how often were they truly sincere?

"Sorry," I mumbled (again).

Steve looked at Mom. "Actually, I might as well just go back to my house today. We're in a holding pattern until we hear back from the SBI lab."

"True. No reason to stay around here." I walked to the freezer, took out a couple of frozen dinners, and shoved them in his direction. "Consider these a gift."

"Um, thanks." Steve awkwardly took the frost-bitten boxes. "I'm sorry you've had to sleep on the couch. But hey, maybe they'll finish with the forensic stuff early."

Usually, this would be the kind of optimism that would enthuse me. But not that day. Not from him.

"You really don't know anything about forensics, do you? The heat from the fire probably destroyed all the marrow. We're not going to learn anything from them. We'll never know who was buried out there!"

"Oh? Well… um." Steve looked around for a place to set his frozen dinners. "I'll be out of here in a few minutes. I'd like to take the McFarland file back to my house."

"I'll get it," I said.

He turned to Mom, "Angela, it's really nice of you to let me stay here. I'll make it up to you. I promise."

Mom smiled. "I may just take you up on that."

I gagged as I walked into my bedroom.

Mom asked, "Why does Boo—Hank have that file?"

From my bedroom doorway, I glared at Steve and shook my head.

Steve looked at me and then back at Mom. "I gave it to him to hide here just in case anyone went through my house."

"Oh." That answer satisfied her.

AFTER I GOT RID of Steve, I went to Hannah's house to see how last night's monitoring went, and to check on her progress with the sticky note.

Hannah answered the door, grabbed my hand, and yanked me up the stairs.

She bounced on her heels. "Guess what!"

"You have to go to the bathroom?" I asked.

"No."

"Did Buckley get an important phone call?"

"No. The man has absolutely no friends. He hasn't made or received a single call. Telemarketers don't even want to talk to him!"

"Did you find Stacy McFarland buried in your basement?" I asked.

"No! Jeez you suck at guessing!" she said. "I cracked the sticky note code!"

"Really?"

"I stayed up most of the night and combed through every online dictionary and translation website I could find until I had multiple possible-translations of each word, word-pair or phrase and then I tried pairing anything together that would make sense. *Thuc dieu* translates into 'the thing' and *Nhot nhat con gai* can translate into 'knotty girl.' So, the sticky note says: 'the thing is in knotty girl.'"

"Okay?" I asked.

"Don't you remember... at Fripp's Graveyard—the boat named *Knotty Girl*?"

"You think the note says that something is in the boat named *Knotty Girl* at Fripp's Graveyard?"

"Obviously," she answered.

36

The state of North Carolina defines criminal trespass as intentionally entering or staying on someone else's property without permission. The element of intent is meant to prevent a criminal charge for accidentally entering someone else's property. For more details see Forensics 411 episode 12, "Crossing the Line."

THERE WAS no point in arguing with Hannah. She was sure that her translation referred to a boat.

We got to the boatyard before lunchtime. It was a hot Saturday in July. People swamped the marina and boat ramp looking to maximize their weekend fun with beer and bait. That made it easy to make our move unnoticed.

"I think *Knotty Girl* was back that way." She pointed.

"You realize that this isn't the only boatyard in existence, right?"

"It's not?"

I wasn't sure whether she was joking. "Plus, there's the possibility that we're not looking for a boat *at all*."

"Aren't you all Mr. Positive?" she said with a snarky expression.

"Hey, you kids—get out of here! This is private property! Didn't you see the signs?"

Hannah turned to find the voice and for some reason walked toward it rather than away. I followed.

She approached the bald, tattooed man and said, "Oh, I'm sorry sir. Are you the owner?"

He wiped his greasy hands on a rag. "Yeah."

"I lost my dog. He's a big St. Bernard. I got a call that someone saw him here."

"Well, I ain't seen a St. Bernard, and you can't be here. It's private property."

"I know. Mozart could die out here if one of these boats fell on him."

She got tears in her eyes. "He was my brother's dog. He died in Afghanistan, you know, serving his country."

Her spellbinding eyes pleaded with him. "I can't lose Mozart. He's all I have left of my brother. Could we please just look for him?"

The man growled. "No! You're trespassing! Get out of here!"

Hannah put her hands to her face, and her shoulders shook. "Please? We'll be fast."

"Get out of here, or I'm calling the cops!" He reached in his pocket for his phone.

I put my hands up. "Fine. Sorry. We're leaving." I grabbed Hannah's hand.

She wiped real tears from her eyes as I pulled her away.

"Mozart! Here boy! Mozart!" Under her breath, she said, "We'll come back tonight."

I whispered, "Your brother died in Afghanistan?"

She blushed and shook her head. "No, I was just making that up to get the guy to feel sorry for me. I'm an excellent actress."

"You were very believable," I said.

"You should've seen my portrayal of the third Little Pig in second grade. I stole the show!"

HANNAH'S DECLARATION that her brother died got me thinking. After parting ways with her at the intersection between our houses, I decided it was time to do some research. I knew that Hannah's family moved from Pittsburgh, that she had attended Millview Elementary, and that something terrible had happened to her in fifth grade. She may or may not have had a brother who died in Afghanistan.

I typed "Simmons, death, Pittsburgh, Millview Elementary," a quintet of generic words that could produce millions of unrelated results. The search engine took 1.6 seconds to produce 1.7 million hits. I clicked on the first one and read.

37

I n a criminal investigation, an investigator may have more than one
possible explanation for how a crime occurred. They might prefer
one interpretation over another and then overvalue evidence or interpret evidence in a way that confirms their chosen explanation for how
the crime unfolded. This is known as confirmation bias. See Forensics
411 episode 13, "Looking for Clues."

READY? Hannah texted. I'm outside.

It was close to midnight. Fog rolled in so thick that I couldn't
see her waiting at the bottom of the steps off the back porch.

After reading the articles from the *Pittsburgh Gazette*, I was
dumbfounded. Hannah had a history I knew nothing about... a
bad history. I had so many questions about her brother and the
woman named Helen Tate, but I didn't know where to begin.

"I worked on the translations some more. I'm confident that
I'm right. It makes sense."

"For our purposes," I added.

She stopped pushing her bike and looked at me. "What do
you mean?"

"I think you have a case of confirmation bias."

"Tell me, *Forensics 411* Detective, what's that? I'm dying to know."

"It's when humans naturally tend to interpret new information so that it confirms their pre-existing beliefs. Like when we found the skeleton on Pelican Island and you jumped to the conclusion that it was Stacy McFarland. Corker said it seemed like too much of a coincidence that we would be investigating the McFarland case, and then suddenly find her body. He was suggesting that we might be experiencing confirmation bias."

Hannah got on her bike. "Oh really, is that what he was suggesting?"

"If you don't believe me, you can Google it."

"Let's just go." She rode ahead of me, so fast I had to pedal quickly to keep up.

We didn't talk on the way to the boatyard. When we got there, the locked chain link fence was a minor obstacle. "We'll have to go over," I said.

As she made her way over the eight-foot fence, I said, "Look, I'm sorry. I didn't mean to burst your bubble, but it makes zero sense that someone would leave a note inside the McFarland file saying, 'the thing is in *Knotty Girl*.' Why would someone hide anything related to the McFarland case in a random boat? And we don't know what 'the thing' even is."

From the top, she lowered herself down the inside of the fence. "It also doesn't make any sense that the file we got from the police station is a photocopy—but it is!"

"Okay, so following your suspicion that something related to the McFarland file is hidden in the boat called *Knotty Girl*, *what* would be hidden and *who* put it there?"

She stopped walking, put her hands on her hips and said, "I never said I had *all* the answers!"

I opened my mouth to say something, but decided against it.

Instead, I pointed toward the back of the boatyard. "*Knotty Girl* is back that way." But then I turned a circle. "Wait, I don't know, it's so foggy I can't get my bearings."

"This way."

"Not that I'm buying into this whole object-hidden-in-a-boat theory, but I happened to find some information about *Knotty Girl* on the Fripp's Boatyard website. She's a 1956 34-foot day cruiser, abandoned since 1969. Old Man Fripp is selling her for 800 dollars."

Hannah turned and looked at me. The fog was making her hair quickly expand. "Sounds like you don't think my idea is that far-fetched if you researched the boat."

"I was curious, that's all."

Knotty Girl rested at an angle on her port side, so the starboard side tilted higher as if she were about to sink on dry land. "I'll get a ladder," I said.

I returned with one we'd passed on the way in, propped it against the stern and climbed aboard. "Be careful where you walk. The boat could have dry rot, and you could fall straight through the hull which could be infested with rats."

"Great," Hannah said. "Rats are my favorite rodent—so much better than guinea pigs. I've always thought guinea pigs were overrated. And don't even get me started on hamsters!"

The back end of the boat wasn't enclosed. "Man!"

"What?" Hannah peeked over the stern.

"This boat is all wood. You don't see that anymore." I went to the cockpit. Rats or rot had destroyed the cushions, carpet, and electronic wires. "I call my boat a 'classic,' but this one really is! She was a real beauty at one time."

I ran my hand slowly along the dusty dashboard, picturing it clean with a shiny coat of varnish.

Hannah sniggered, "Should I leave you two alone?"

I pulled my hand back and said, "You check the built-in storage in the stern area. I'll inspect the cabin."

"Which part is the stern again?" she asked.

"The back, check the back."

While I went through the interior cabin, I heard her pulling open trap doors and storage hatches.

"Hannah! Get in here!"

She scrambled in behind me. "What'd you find?"

I handed her a grimy leather-bound book.

She opened it and started reading. "I told you! *Never* doubt a woman's intuition!" She did a little jig and practically squealed her words, "This isn't some random boat, it's the Buckley's!"

We looked at Bob Buckley Sr.'s signature at the bottom of each page of the captain's log, then pulled the cabin apart piece by piece looking for anything linked to Stacy McFarland.

"Nothing," I grunted.

Hannah said, "Come outside. There's a trap door I can't open. I need your help."

The door built into the floorboards had a round ring that you had to turn and pull up to open. "Let me see if I can find a screwdriver or something."

"Oh, there was a crowbar in one of those storage places on the side."

I found what she was talking about and chuckled. "You're such a city-girl! This is a gaff. You use it to grab a big fish that you've got hooked."

"Well, it'll work, won't it?"

"We can try." I stuck the gaff hook through the ring handle of the hatch and yanked with all my might, but it didn't budge.

"Let me try," Hannah said, nudging me to the side.

"Have at it, `GirlofSteel`!" I handed her the gaff.

Of course, she got it on the first try.

"That's not storage," Hannah said, looking inside the hatch.

We aimed our flashlights into the cavity. "That's the inboard motor," I said. I lay down on my stomach to get a better look.

"See anything?" she asked.

"Shine your light over there." I pointed.

"What do you see?"

"Gaff," I said, sticking my hand out over my shoulder as if I were a doctor asking for a surgical instrument.

She handed it to me, and I used it to reach into the space around the engine. It was about three feet deep. I hung over the side of the motor well as far as I could, then raked the gaff into the depths of the cavity. "I've got something!" I called, moving around to the other corner of the hatch opening. "I just can't reach it."

"I'll hold your legs," she said.

I stretched as far as I could, and felt it again. "Hold on tight. I need to be lower," I said.

Finally, I made contact and used the hooked end of the gaff to drag the object along the bottom of the engine well. I leaned in even more, snagged the item with my hand and passed it over my shoulder to Hannah. It was flat and felt like a book.

"Oh, my gosh!" Hannah said, letting go of my legs. I plummeted forward, hitting my head on the top of the engine.

"What the crap!" I yelled.

"Oh, sorry. Are you okay?" She reached under my arms and pulled me backward.

I sat back on my legs and reached for my forehead to feel for a lump.

"Ooh, you're bleeding."

I pulled my hand away and looked at it. "Do I need stitches?"

She pulled her sleeve down over her hand and used it to blot away the blood on my face. "No, you big baby, you don't need stitches. It's not that bad."

She put her hands on my shoulders and pulled me toward her. "I'll make it all better." Then she leaned in and kissed my forehead.

"There." She patted me on the shoulder. "All better?"

I nodded slowly.

Hannah sat back on her legs. "Sorry I dropped you, but check this out!"

She held a large, filthy brown envelope, about two inches thick.

I sat beside her as she opened it. Inside was what appeared to be the original McFarland file. It contained some of the same things we had already seen copies of, like the list of missing items. But it also held pages and pages of relevant information the folder from the station had not.

I skimmed them. "Mr. Parker, Stacy's next-door neighbor, said he saw a beat-up white van pass the McFarland house a couple of times, and that it was later parked at the pool."

Hannah flipped the page and I read over her shoulder.

"Holy crap! They did a luminol test in the McFarland's garage and found traces of blood on the tool bench."

"Is that the stuff from TV that turns blue?" she asked.

"Yes. It's called chemiluminescence, and the effect happens when you spray luminol on blood. It even works on dried or cleaned-up blood. Let me see it." I pulled the file out of her hands.

"Hey!" Hannah said, "How about using your manners!"

"Sorry," I said turning to the next page of the file. "Here's the lab order to test a sample from the McFarland's garage."

Hannah pointed. "But where are the results?"

"Hmm," I flipped through the pages that followed. "There aren't any."

"No, wait," Hannah said. "Right here in the report, Bob Buckley says that the sample taken from the garage was actually bleach."

"That happens sometimes. Bleach can show up as chemiluminescent, too. But it's possible that someone purposely cleaned the tool bench with bleach to cover traces of blood that might have been there. You know, like the burglar," I said. "Do you see the actual lab results?"

Hannah said, "Look, here's the map of where they searched. According to this, Buckley searched the woods near my house. How did he not find the bracelet?"

"It's like he didn't want to solve the case," I answered.

I skimmed down the page looking for mention of Mr. McFarland's car. "Yes!" I said, making a celebratory fist pump. "There's a note that says that Mr. McFarland's car door was unlocked when the police came to investigate. That means the burglar could have definitely used the automatic garage door opener to get in the house."

Hannah shook her head. "It doesn't look like the journal's in here." Then she touched my arm, "Wait, there are pictures of the journal pages, though." She looked closer, her curly hair brushing against my shoulder.

She took the file from my hands. "Oh my god, you have got to be kidding! This thing is wrong on so many levels." She clucked her tongue and pointed at the journal photos.

"First of all, this doesn't look like a girl's handwriting at all. It's too sloppy, and it's not puffy. It's all capital letters. Girls don't write like that. Girl-writing is usually bubbly. It's something we actually practice."

I scooted closer, breathing in the scent of her hair.

"Secondly, she doesn't write anything about what happened at school. She only says how much she likes getting high and how much she hates her parents. She doesn't even say *why* she hates them. That's weird. Most people use a journal to sort through their feelings, not just write them down."

"You're going down the confirmation bias rabbit hole. We suspect the journal is a fake and that Stacy didn't write it, so maybe you're interpreting things to fit our suspicions rather than just examining the evidence for what it is."

"Fine," she answered, not convinced. "But we can get these pictures to Mrs. McFarland and see if she thinks it looks like Stacy's handwriting. Officer Corker can help us with that."

"If the journal is a fake, we still don't know *why* someone made it or what happened to Stacy," Hannah said.

"I think Buckley made it because he wanted to close the case, so he could say he solved it. The best way to do that was to say

Stacy ran away. And, don't forget, we might know what happened to Stacy if it turns out that the bones from the campfire are her."

"That can tell us if she died, but we still won't know how or why."

38

Associative evidence is evidence that ties a suspect to the crime scene. A few examples are fingerprints, hair, fibers, and bodily fluids. For more information see Forensics 411 *episode 1, "The Basics."*

BY THE NEXT MORNING, I had read through the entire file three times. Around ten, Hannah texted me with a wiretap report: #nothing #mostboringjobever #manhasnofriends

Just as I was about to respond, the doorbell rang.

"Oh, look, the Casanova Cop's back," I said as I opened the door.

He ignored my dig. "We're still working this case, aren't we?"

I motioned him in as his phone rang.

After he answered it, he covered the mouthpiece and said, "It's the DNA results."

I scrambled over to the kitchen table. He put the phone on speaker and set it on the table so I could listen.

The forensic pathologist said, "I'm not sure how, but I got enough of a DNA sample from the bone to build a profile. Unfortunately, I can't give you a positive ID. It didn't match anything in CODIS. However, it *did* match DNA found in traces of blood droplets on the fabric you gave me. That means the bone belongs to someone who bled on the fabric. I can also tell you that the bone was part of the left arm of a Caucasian woman, under the age of twenty. She broke the arm prior to death, but it had healed. The young lady had type AB negative blood, which is the rarest. The bone is forty to fifty years old." He took a breath. "With the information I have, I can't say that the bone belonged to Stacy McFarland, but it *could have*. I'd need a sample of her DNA for comparison to be sure. I have a report with all my findings, but those are the major points that might help you. Do you have an email address where I can send you everything?"

Steve gave him his personal email address and added, "Do *not* send it to the Vista Point police."

The forensic pathologist continued, "The news on the Coke bottle is more definitive. Again, we were lucky to get a DNA sample that hadn't been too degraded. We built a profile, and there's a match in CODIS: A guy named Monty St. Clair. He's eighty years old, lives in the Georgia Department of Corrections in DeKalb County, and is serving time for robbery, vagrancy, and continual probation violations. His record dates back to the late sixties for theft, check fraud, and burglary."

"Is there any indication that he was ever in North Carolina?"

"Yes. Cops charged him with contributing to the delinquency of a minor in Wilmington on May 25, 1985. He bought beer for some teenagers, and the cashier reported him."

After thanking the pathologist, Steve hung up.

We looked at each other.

"An arrest in May 1985 puts him in the area near the time that Stacy disappeared," I said.

"And the DNA puts him in the woods beside Stacy's house. We've got some dots to connect."

"Let's call Connie McFarland," Steve said. "She'll know Stacy's blood type and whether she ever broke her left arm."

"What about Monty St. Clair?" I asked. "Don't we need to follow up on that?"

Grandpa came in the kitchen. "Monty St. Clair? I haven't heard that name in years! Your snooping has turned up more drunks than a race ticket giveaway in Daytona!"

We turned to Grandpa.

"You know Monty St. Clair?"

"He used to hang out at the Purple Pelican with Arthur Buckley. Just another Vista Point bum."

And another Buckley connection.

STEVE REACHED Connie McFarland in no time. After explaining who we were and what we'd learned, we got the information we needed from Mrs. McFarland.

Stacy had broken her arm in ninth grade in a cheerleading accident and had type AB negative blood.

"You know," Mrs. McFarland said, "she wasn't the miserable drug addict that the police made her out to be. She was popular and got good grades. She was beautiful inside and out."

Steve explained our investigation and the DNA results. He didn't mention that the skeleton we'd found had been severely damaged by fire.

"Based on what the pathologist said, the remains *could* be Stacy," Steve said. "Nothing in the DNA profile excludes her. But we need a sample of her DNA to say for sure. Do you happen to have something that would contain her DNA?"

We heard a sniffle from the other end of the call.

I jotted a note on a piece of paper and slid it across the table.

"I don't think so," she answered with disappointment. "She was born in 1969. It's not like I preserved her umbilical cord, like these weird parents today."

Steve read my note, nodded, and gave me the thumbs up.

"Did you happen to keep any of her things like a hairbrush or her toothbrush?"

"I have everything in the attic," she answered. "Part of me has always hoped that the police were right, that she ran away, and that one day she would just show up again."

"You're in Raleigh, right?"

"Yes."

Steve arranged for Mrs. McFarland to take Stacy's toothbrush and hairbrush to the state crime lab there. "I'll call ahead and notify the lab that you're coming. A representative will meet you at whatever time you can be there," Steve said.

"Thank you, officer. I really appreciate your interest in finding out the truth about my Stacy. The rest of those Vista Point cops never seemed to care."

"Yes, ma'am. Thank you." He hung up.

Steve looked at me. "I need to call Brian and see if he's back in Raleigh to meet Mrs. McFarland."

It turned out that Brian was still in Vista Point trying to track down Chief Buckley, but Agent Horton would be able to meet her.

Over the speaker, I heard Agent Watts say, "I'm working with a judge to get a warrant to search Chester Buckley's personal property. I'd like to find the guys who posed as the CSI team, but based on your descriptions, it sounds like their most memorable feature was their body odor. I've been to the police station twice, and most of the Vista Point police seem to be on vacation this week. It's crazy. I keep getting the run-around, and no one has seen Chief Buckley in a couple of days."

Steve filled Agent Watts in on the connection between the New Coke bottle DNA, Monty St. Clair, and the fact that he was in the area in 1985.

Watts said, "Agent Horton can get in touch with the Georgia Bureau of Investigation. They'll send someone to question St. Clair. If he refuses to talk, the GBI will have to get a subpoena and a public defender to sit in on the questioning with him. That could take a while. I'll keep you posted."

"Thanks, man. Bye."

Steve got up. "I'm going to head into the station and see what's going on."

39

Police need a warrant to search private property. However, they don't need a warrant to search public areas, and a police station is a public property. All you need is a way into the building. See Forensics 411 *episode 13, "Search and Seizure."*

HANNAH CAME to my house at about seven-thirty in the morning.

"So, Officer Corker went back to work yesterday?" she asked.

"I think he went right after we got the news about the DNA. I wonder if he could get in the database? I'd love to learn more about Monty St. Clair."

"Did you try calling him?"

"Monty St. Clair?" I asked.

"No, Steve."

"Yeah. I called him four times yesterday, and he didn't get back to me."

She said, "I really think we need to send the photos of the skeleton to the press. It's not right that no one even knows about the body you and Chaucer found. You know? Somebody died. Their life meant something."

"That's true. But I worry about the trial. We don't want to

mess things up for the prosecution by making the photos public."

"The photos are your property. You can do whatever you want with them. My dad said so. And I think it's clear that the cops aren't trying to figure out who that body was. The person buried on Pelican Island deserves to be acknowledged as having lived and died."

"I guess." I took my phone off my nightstand. "Let's try Corker again and see what he says."

I hung up. "Voicemail again."

Hannah got excited. "Let's do it! Let's send the photos to the media. We can hit everyone from the *Vista Point Voice* to the *Charlotte Examiner* and all the TV stations in between. Once the photos are out there, the cops won't be able to deny that the skeleton existed and they're going to have to answer questions."

I agreed, though a bit reluctantly.

Hannah wrote a Pulitzer-worthy summary of when and where we found the skeleton. We didn't mention anything related to Stacy McFarland. It was enough to get the information out that the body we'd found had disappeared. The news media would start calling Chief Buckley for details, and things would get moving.

The last email went to Chief Buckley from one of my anonymous accounts. Under the photo of the skeleton, Hannah typed:

Did you lose the skeleton on the way to the crime lab? - Forensics 411 Detective and WhoDunnitHannah

"WhoDunnitHannah?" I asked, reading over her shoulder.

"You like it?"

She beamed at me. "I figure I need a screen name that's more relevant than `GirlofSteel`. You *are* going to make a *Forensics 411* segment about our investigation, aren't you?"

"Of course," I answered, having only dreamt that Hannah would want to be a part of it. "But, don't sign our names. We don't want Chief Buckley to know that we're the ones with the photos."

"Shouldn't that be obvious?" Hannah asked. "Who else would've been able to photograph the skeleton in the ground?"

"Not everything is obvious to Chief Buckley."

She hit send and continued. "I've got a few production ideas for the McFarland episode."

As she went on about her ideas for *Forensics 411*, I basked in the indescribable joy of "me" being part of a "we" for the first time in my life.

Hannah's tablet beeped. Chief Buckley was getting a call. It was the first one since we'd placed the tap on his line.

We looked at each other with wide eyes as we heard him say "hello" in his southern drawl.

"Chief Buckley?"

"Yes," he answered.

"This is Dr. Powell's office calling to remind you that you have a dental appointment at 4 p.m. on Wednesday."

"I'll be there. Thanks." He hung up.

"At least we know the tap works," Hannah said, then added, "Hey, did you give Officer Corker the original file we found in the boat?" Hannah asked.

"Not yet."

"We should probably take it to him. He's back at work, right?"

"He's supposed to be."

Just as I stood to get the original McFarland file from my closet, Hannah's tablet beeped again. This time Chief Buckley was making a call.

HANNAH and I huddled over the tablet, listening to Chester's conversation.

"Bob? It's Chester, we've got trouble!"

"I know. I just got the email you forwarded to me," the mayor answered.

Chester said, "I can't figure how anyone would get a picture of that skeleton, but it sure looks like the one from the island. Same position. Same sand. Same hole."

"You idiot! It's got to be the Boyd boy. Who else would've known about it?"

"Oh yeah, I guess that makes sense. All these kids have phones with cameras."

"So, when you were with him on the island you didn't *ask* him if he took any pictures?"

"Look, you told me to get them off the island as fast as possible. I did. You told me to get rid of the skeleton, and I did. I sent Corker to Bollywood, and Rodney fixed it so Corker couldn't get into the computer system. Corker was supposed to be back yesterday but didn't show. He'll want to know about the identity of the skeleton, and he'll probably try to log into the computer system."

"Corker won't be in today," Mayor Buckley said.

Hannah and I looked at each other.

"Why?" Chester asked.

"Nothing you need to worry about," the mayor answered.

"I've also got that Watts fella from the SBI snooping around. Marcia said he was at the station yesterday wanting to see the file on the McFarland girl that disappeared back in the eighties. She told him she already sent it to permanent storage. Then Marcia told me that JoAnn Lubbock told *her* that after Corker got back from Pelican Island, *he* was looking for the McFarland file, too. Do those bones on the island have something to do with that girl?" Chester asked.

Bob said, "Just stay away from Watts. I'm working on getting another skeleton to show him."

"I asked you a question!" Chester said. "Does that skeleton have anything to do with the McFarland case?"

"Drop it, Chester!" Bob insisted. "Avoid that SBI fella for as long as you can. Don't go to work. Tell Marcia you're sick. Don't answer your phone unless it's from me."

"No!" Chester argued. "I want answers. I've done all this crap for you without question because you told me to trust you. But it seems like you're getting me in deeper and deeper trouble. I'm sick of it! If you don't tell me what's really going on, I'm gonna...." Chester's voice drifted off.

"You're going to *what*?"

"I'm gonna quit helping you. That's what!" Chester sounded like a six-year-old.

"Fine!" Bob said. "It was Arthur."

Hannah gasped. I leaned in closer to the tablet.

"Arthur?" Chester asked. "Those bones are Arthur? Arthur's dead?"

"No, you moron! Arthur's alive. I saw him last week, drunk as a skunk," Bob said. "Look, that skeleton might be the McFarland girl, and the last thing we need is for *her* to turn up after all these years! I've got a re-election campaign to worry about. You do, too. It's hard to get re-elected with a murderer in the family."

"But that girl ran away. You said so yourself. You found that journal. You closed the case."

Mayor Buckley didn't respond.

After a moment of silence, Chester said, "You mean to tell me that you had me destroy the skeleton so that you didn't get embarrassed because you thought the girl ran away, but she really didn't?"

"No, you half-wit! She didn't run away. Arthur robbed the house. He took the girl and did something to her. I think he killed her, and that might've been her on the island."

"How do you know?"

Silence.

"Tell me!" Chester demanded.

"A couple of days after the McFarland girl disappeared, Arthur called me and told me his van was missing. I went over to his apartment. It was Friday, but he thought it was Wednesday. He had been passed out since Tuesday. The girl disappeared on a *Tuesday* night. Arthur was limping, and all beat up. His shirt had blood splattered on it. He wanted me to file a theft report on the van so Pop wouldn't think he'd lost it like he did that other car. I had him write down a description of the car and told him I'd take care of it. Only, I didn't. I was so bogged down with the McFarland case. The press was hounding me. The girl's mother wouldn't leave me alone. I didn't know what I was doing. It's not like I'd ever investigated a murder or kidnapping before. So, that day I shoved the description of Arthur's van in my pocket and forgot about it until I picked up my uniform from the dry cleaners the next week. That's when I looked at the description. Arthur's vehicle was a white 1974 Ford Econoline cargo van with a dent in the back of the driver's side."

"Sure, I remember it."

"The Parker fella that lived next door to the McFarlands told me he saw a white cargo van with a dent on the driver's side pass his house *twice* on the night of the robbery. *And* he saw it parked at the neighborhood pool later that night, but it was gone the next morning. That was Arthur's van."

"I don't remember hearing anything about a van back then," Chester said.

"I buried it. I didn't let it get out to the press. Then I told Mr. Parker that I'd tracked down the owner of the van and he was doing some repairs at the pool after hours." Bob continued. "Arthur couldn't account for where he had been on Wednesday and Thursday of the week that the girl disappeared. He looked like he'd been in a fight. He told me he'd been playing cards with the fellas from the Purple Pelican, and that they figured out he was cheating, and roughed him up. But I questioned his buddies over there. Every single one of them said they had *never* played cards with him at his apartment. And none of them had seen him for a few days around the time of the girl's disappearance."

"That doesn't mean he robbed and killed the McFarland girl.

And do you honestly think the guys from the Purple Pelican would tell a cop that they beat up his brother?"

"Arthur had blood on his shirt, but it was splattered on the front, which means it wasn't his. It came from someone else who was standing in front of him. I found traces of blood in the McFarland's garage."

"I don't remember hearing about any blood."

"I made sure it never came out," Bob said.

"The guys from the Purple Pelican could've lied to you about beating up Arthur. And Arthur has a history of disappearing. Remember when he called you from Myrtle Beach that time? He had no idea how he got there or where the five hundred bucks in his wallet came from," Chester said. "Did you *ask* him if he killed the girl?"

"No, I didn't *ask* him! It's not as if he would've told me the truth! He might have been so drunk that he didn't even know he did it! You know he blacks out. I was better off not asking. What if he said he'd killed her?"

"Well, ya could've covered for him!" Chester answered sarcastically. "Oh wait, you did that anyway!"

"I guess that's right," Bob grumbled. "I just preferred not to hear what he'd done to that poor girl."

"So, all these years, you've been covering for him and never even bothered to ask him if he did it?" Chester asked.

"Yes."

"And you think those bones from the island are the McFarland girl?"

"They *could* be."

"And you never told anyone about this?"

"I told Pop, only because I didn't know what to do. He was the one who came up with the idea of making it look like she ran away."

"What about the diary you found?"

"For Pete's sake, Chester, I made that up! Pop said we had to cover for Arthur. That's what family does. Since there was no sign of forced entry, no sign of a struggle according to my report, it was easy to make it look like she ran away."

"Then it wasn't an accident that the diary disappeared from the evidence room at the station before the girl's parents could see it?"

"No, I took it from the records room and destroyed it. Then I hid the real McFarland report and replaced it with a dummy report."

Hannah and I looked at each other.

"I see," Chester said. "And since you told me to burn that skeleton, we'll never know whether that body was the McFarland girl or not."

"That's the plan," Bob answered.

"What am I supposed to do?" Chester asked. "The SBI fella is going to want to see the skeleton, and I don't have one to show him."

"Like I said, I'm working on getting another skeleton. Just lay low until I call you. Stay away from the station, the press, and that SBI fella." The line went dead.

"Arthur Buckley killed Stacy McFarland!" Hannah said.

"And Bob was the one that figured it out and has been covering for him all these years—not Chester!"

"Wow! He wasn't incompetent—he was a dirty cop! And now he's done something to Steve."

I stood up. "If the mayor's trying to eliminate people who know the truth, we could be next. We need to move fast."

"But he doesn't know that *we* know about Arthur," Hannah argued. "And they don't know we got the DNA sample from the bones."

"Let's try to call Corker again," I said.

40

Typically, burglars take 8-12 minutes to rob a home. The things they are most likely to steal are cash, tools, jewelry, wallets or purses, guns, video games, game consoles, and laptops or tablets. The most burglaries occur between 10:00 a.m. and 3:00 p.m. See Forensics 411 _episode 15, "Property Crimes."_

OUR CALL WENT straight to Steve's voice mail.

I grabbed a backpack from my closet, put Hannah's tablet in it so we could continue to monitor Chief Buckley's calls, then we set off for Steve's.

We cut through the woods below Hannah's house and parked our bikes beside his car in the rear driveway. Everything was quiet, but the back door was standing open, and the glass was shattered.

Hannah whispered, "My parents told me that if I ever came home and the door was wide open, I shouldn't go in. You're supposed to go to a neighbor's house and call the police."

"I don't know that the police are going to be much help with this," I answered.

"What about Agent Watts? We could call him," Hannah suggested.

I pulled my boomerang from the waistband of my shorts and brandished it like a weapon, prepared to pummel someone if necessary. "Let's just go in. If Mayor Buckley did something to Steve, he did it before he talked to Chester on the phone this morning. If someone was here, they're probably long gone."

"*Probably?*" Hannah asked. "I don't like those odds."

I walked toward the open back door. "Watch the glass on the floor," I said.

The broken glass was only the beginning. The drawers and cabinets of the kitchen hung open. Food from the freezer and refrigerator covered the countertops. The couch cushions were on the floor, and desk drawers were empty. Same with his bedroom. Noticeably, his phone, wallet, and gun were still on the nightstand.

"If this were a robbery, they would've taken his wallet and gun," I whispered.

"Maybe they were looking for the McFarland file," Hannah said as she scanned the room.

"I bet Agent Watts's number is in Steve's phone." I picked it up and searched the recent calls. Brian Watts had called Corker thirty minutes before.

I dialed his number and got his voice mail.

"Agent Watts, this is Hank Boyd calling from Steve Corker's phone. He's gone, and we think Bob Buckley took him. Yes, that's *Bob* Buckley, not *Chester*. But we found out that Chester did burn the skeleton, and he did it because Bob told him to. Bob says that their younger brother, *Arthur*, was the one that robbed the McFarlands and killed Stacy. We're at Steve's house right now."

"Now what?" Hannah asked after I'd hung up. She took out her phone, while I checked mine.

"I've got emails from the *Vista Point Voice, Wilmington*

Observer, and *WBCH News.* Everybody's interested in the skeleton, and they want to talk to us."

"We're kind of busy for a press junket, don't you think?"

"Not if the media can help us," I said. "Let's tell them that Officer Corker is missing, and we suspect that his disappearance is connected to the skeleton. We can splatter Steve's face all over Twitter, Facebook, Instagram and send his picture to all the news outlets."

I handed Hannah her tablet so she could spread the news of Steve's disappearance to the local media. Then I opened Steve's wallet and removed his driver's license, holding it out to Hannah. "Take a picture of this so we can include it with the emails and tweets."

41

S tate and local law enforcement agencies are not subordinate to the FBI, and the FBI does not "take over" local cases. Instead local and state investigators pool efforts with the FBI to solve cases. See Forensics 411 episode 14, "Who's in Charge?"

THANKFULLY, Agent Watts called me back on Steve's phone within a few minutes.

"What's going on?" he asked.

"Hannah and I are at Steve's house. The door was wide open, and his place was ransacked."

"In your message, you said *Arthur Buckley* robbed the McFarland's and Bob's been covering for him all these years? How do you know that?"

"We overheard a conversation between Chester and Bob," I answered. "Steve's missing, and we're pretty sure Bob Buckley took him."

"So, we have a kidnapper mayor, a body-burning police chief, and they've got a possible thief and murderer for a brother? Nice family." Agent Watts scoffed. "I'm at the police station. It's locked up tight, and there's no one here. I've called the Special Services wing of the SBI to come in and act as local law enforcement. What's Steve's address? I'm coming to get you."

We sat on Steve's mattress on the floor. Hannah was sending out tweets and emails to the media when we heard a car skid to a stop in the gravel driveway.

"That's probably Agent Watts," Hannah said, getting up to meet him while I finished my post on my *Forensics 411* page.

I clicked "post" just before Hannah screamed.

In the kitchen, a masked man had Hannah. He was attempting to drag her out the back door, but she kicked and tried to wrestle her way out of his grip. She looked terrified.

Adrenaline took over. I ran back to Steve's bedroom, glanced at the gun, but grabbed my boomerang. The man was outside with Hannah, pulling her toward his car. I catapulted myself through the back door and aimed the boomerang as best I could.

"Watch out!" I yelled to Hannah as I threw the boomerang from Steve's porch and prayed it hit its mark. Wind, elevation, layover, spin—there were so many factors to consider when throwing a boomerang. It wasn't something I usually threw at a target.

The masked man's hand momentarily slipped from Hannah's mouth. She let out a primal scream and dove to the left slamming onto the gravel with her hands out in front of her.

The leading wing of my boomerang nailed the guy's head. He crumbled to the ground. I gathered Hannah from the driveway and shoved her toward the house while the masked man pulled himself up the side of Steve's car.

"Go!" I screamed.

The attacker got back to his feet and lunged at me. He was big. My only advantage would be speed and turning radius. I ran around to the front of the car where my boomerang had ricocheted. I palmed one wing, planning to hammer him with it. He placed one massive hand on my face and gave me a strong push backward while he ripped the boomerang from my hand with the other. I crashed to the ground on my back, getting the wind knocked out of my lungs.

He stood above me and grunted. I used my legs to squirm backward on the gravel. Each pebble grated along my spine as I tried to wriggle away. This was it! I was going to die! Some guy in a mask was going to murder me with a blunt force trauma to the head. It would be the perfect subject for a *Forensics 411* episode, only I wouldn't be around to make it. I'd be starring as "Victim #1."

"Hank! Get out of the way!" Hannah yelled. I turned toward her voice.

She was standing on the porch with Steve's gun pointed at us.

The man turned from me and lunged toward Hannah. I got on all fours and crawled behind the car as I watched his massive body sail through the air in slow-motion, like an attacking animal on one of those wildlife documentaries. Hannah stepped backward, her eyes getting bigger as I heard a gunshot. And then another. I closed my eyes as my body slammed back onto the gravel.

42

Post-Traumatic Stress Disorder may develop after a terrifying experience. Symptoms can include irritability, aggression, trouble sleeping, panic attacks, becoming emotionally numb, and in some cases selective mutism. See Forensics 411 episode 32, "Understanding the Victim."

I MUST HAVE PASSED OUT, then woke on the ground to the sound of crying. Disoriented, I sat up and looked at my throbbing hands, embedded with gravel. Hannah was standing on the porch, holding the gun, her whole body shaking violently.

I followed her gaze to the masked man. Agent Watts was standing above him with his gun drawn. Our attacker was bleeding from his leg. Watts sat him up. While putting handcuffs on the attacker, he addressed Hannah. "Miss, you need to set the gun on the porch and walk away."

She didn't move.

"Miss, set the gun down and walk away."

She shook her head. "I-I c-can't."

He shot a look in my direction, silently asking for my help before the situation exploded.

I inched my way across the driveway and used the railing on the back steps to pull myself to Hannah. She looked at me with terror on her face.

My voice trembled. "Hannah, p-put the gun down."

She shook her head. "I-I c-can't."

"Please set the gun down. We don't want anyone to get hurt," Watts said.

I leaned toward her. "Set the gun down. Okay? He's not going to hurt you. He's handcuffed. You're okay."

Silent tears rolled down her cheeks.

I stood beside her and put a hand on each of her arms and gently directed her downward. She was shaking. "Just sit down. I'm here. Agent Watts is here. Everything's okay."

She looked at Agent Watts while I slowly pried the gun from her fingers. I hadn't held one before, but I knew to keep the barrel facing away from us. I set it on the kitchen counter then, putting twin arms across Hannah's shoulders, I whispered, "It's okay. You're okay."

She rested her head on my shoulder. "I sh-shot him."

"No, if you fired the gun, the barrel would be hot. Agent Watts shot him." The location of his wounds and the angle of the bullet hole in the car meant the shots came from the opposite direction.

Hannah stared into the backyard, nodding. "That's good, right?"

"Yes, that's good," I answered, then squeezed her shoulder.

Agent Watts removed the man's ski mask. "What's your name?" he demanded.

The large man narrowed his beady eyes at Watts, then spat on the driveway in response.

I recognized the face immediately.

"That's Rodney Buckley," I said. "He's related to Chester and Bob Buckley. He's a nephew or great-nephew. He can't talk. Or at least he doesn't talk, not anymore."

Rodney's feral eyes shifted rapidly from side to side as if he were expecting an ambush.

"He used to belong to some survivalist militia group out in Idaho."

"Who sent you here? Where's Steve Corker?" Watts asked.

Rodney answered with a grunt.

Within five minutes, an ambulance, escorted by two state troopers, came and took Rodney away.

Agent Watts made phone call after phone call while Hannah huddled on the back steps, still stunned by the events of our morning. I went inside to use Steve's bathroom and pulled myself together.

As I splashed icy water on my face, Hannah's tablet beeped. Chester Buckley was making or receiving a call.

Agent Watts was on his phone, so I let the tablet record it. When he'd hung up, I called him over to the porch.

"Chief Buckley got another phone call." I pointed to the tablet.

Agent Watts's expression changed. "You said you 'overheard' him talking, you didn't tell me you wiretapped him!" He shook his head. "You know none of the information you've learned from his calls will be admissible in court. How is the prosecutor going to build a case without evidence?"

"It's okay. Bob Buckley made a dummy investigation report on the McFarland case. Corker had the dummy. That's probably what Rodney was after. We have the original. It's got enough in it to implicate Mayor Buckley in a cover-up."

I clicked the "play" icon, and the three of us listened.

"Bob?" Chester said. "I just got a message from Louise Bacon from the *Vista Point Voice*. She was asking about the skeleton from Pelican Island. How do you think she knows about that?"

Mayor Buckley cursed. "That kid must've sent the picture of the skeleton to her. For the love of good, man, why didn't you think to ask the boy if he'd taken any pictures?"

"I already said I'm sorry about that! I didn't think of it.

Louise also asked me if Officer Corker was working today. I didn't know what to say."

"You say, 'no, he's not working today,' you blooming idiot!" Mayor Buckley said.

"You didn't kill him, did you?"

"No, I just had Rodney take him on a field trip. I told my brilliant grandson that we suspected that Corker was part of a terrorist sleeper cell. He's just scaring him a little bit. Rodney has some drug he got from his Idaho buddies that'll make Corker forget that anything ever happened."

His tone changed. "The good news is I got another set of bones, and they're being delivered to the station at one o'clock. It's amazing what you can find on the internet. You need to meet the delivery guy there. It's coming from ShipQuick. Take them out of the packaging. Throw some dirt and sand on the bones and toss them into an evidence bag to make it look like it came from the island. You might want to take a few out, so it doesn't seem like a full set. Take it to the morgue at the hospital and tell the clerk that some peon in the department misplaced the skeletal remains and that you just found them."

"But I'm the coroner. I'm supposed to send the bones to the state crime lab."

"Just play dumb. It should come naturally. Call me after you take the skeleton to the morgue."

"You think it'll work?" Chester asked.

"I managed to keep Arthur's secret for the last thirty years. If we can keep this one for another thirty years, we'll be dead by the time someone figures it out."

"I doubted you for a little bit, but you proved how brilliant you are," Chester said.

"Thanks, little brother. I appreciate it. Now get over to the station so you can meet the ShipQuick guy. And remember, don't let anyone see you."

"Got it!" Chester said.

AGENT WATTS LOOKED at me as I opened my mouth to ask the question.

"Absolutely not! There is no way you're going with me to the police station!"

"But—"

"You've caused enough trouble. And don't even tell me how you put a tap on the police chief's phone," Watts said.

"But we can help," I argued.

"No!" He covered his ears like a defiant child.

43

L aw enforcement officers must file a report each time they discharge their service weapon in the line of duty. See Forensics *411 episode 17, "Wielding Your Weapon."*

I MADE my argument as we got in Watts's car. "You know you have a lot of paperwork to fill out over the shooting incident. Then you'll have to take us home and probably talk to our parents." Mine was at work, but he didn't know that.

Hannah interrupted, "You don't need to say anything to my parents about any of this—*ever!*"

"Seems to me it would make more sense for you to keep us under your protection," I said. "What if someone else comes after us?"

Agent Watts started the engine and looked at me in the rear-view mirror.

"We could just wait in the car."

Hannah clenched her fists. "Take me home. I've had enough."

"Really?" I asked.

"Yes, *really*," she answered with a salty tone. "We aren't cops. We're just kids."

"But we've worked on this all summer. We finally know what happened to Stacy. Arthur Buckley killed her, and Bob covered it up. Don't you want to be there to catch the Buckleys red-handed?"

"No." She took a deep breath. "I almost killed someone today to save you."

I nodded. "I know. That was really nice of you."

She rolled her eyes at me. "Oh, my god, you are so clueless!"

We pulled into Hannah's driveway. She turned to me and shrugged. "I'm sorry. I just..." She reached for the car door.

I wasn't sure what to say. I wished Dr. B had helped me come up with a non-verbal communication strategy that would relay how happy I was that she was safe. I needed a way to tell her that, if necessary, I would've killed Rodney Buckley to protect her.

As I contemplated this, Hannah said, "I gotta go."

She stormed out of the car, across the lawn, and up her front steps.

Agent Watts had his eyes on me in the rearview mirror. "You going after her?"

"Should I?"

"I'm no expert, but don't you think you need to show her she's more important than a police case?"

I shifted my weight around in the back seat. "I don't know. I mean, we worked all summer on this investigation. This is the chance of a lifetime for me."

Agent Watts's cell phone rang as I contemplated what could be the most significant decision of my adolescent life. If I went with Watts, I could be a hero. *Forensics 411* would go viral. But Hannah might not speak to me again. I could lose the only friend I'd ever had.

"Oh, hey Horton. You got my message, huh?" Watts said.

He listened.

"Hang on a minute. I've got the kid right here. He's going to want to hear this."

Watts turned to me. "The forensic pathology team compared the DNA from the radius bone and the blood droplets from the cloth on Pelican Island to the hair samples that the pathologists in Raleigh were able to get from Stacy McFarland's brush. They were a perfect match."

He listened to Agent Horton for about a minute. "Are you kidding me? I sure didn't see *that* coming. Thanks for handling all that."

He hung up and turned to me. "An agent from the Georgia Bureau of Investigation visited Monty St. Clair. As soon as he asked St. Clair if he'd ever been to Vista Point, the guy sang like a canary. He says he and Arthur Buckley used to hang out at some bar and play cards. One night, he and some other fellas from the bar went back to Arthur's to play poker. Arthur was cheating, the fellas figured it out and roughed him up. St. Clair stayed behind after the rest of them left. He planned to rob Arthur. He said Buckley was going on about how he couldn't go to work with his face all messed up because his boss had it out for him. Buckley was a school bus driver."

Watts cleared his throat. "St. Clair told Buckley that he would drive his route the next day for a hundred bucks. He waited until Arthur Buckley passed out, then he stole his cash and took his van. The next day St. Clair drove the morning and afternoon bus routes as promised, and that was going to be it. But on the afternoon route, a girl sitting behind him on the bus was talking about how her parents were out of town, and she was going to a big party that night up the street. He saw the girl's house and a fancy car in the driveway and decided to rob it while the girl was at the party. It was the McFarland's house, and the girl was Stacy."

"So, Arthur *didn't* do it?" I shrugged. "How'd Stacy end up dead?"

"St. Clair says one of the things he stole from the house was a men's gold bracelet, but that he dropped it on his way out. He went back to find it, and Stacy came out into the garage. She had a lawn chair in her hand, dropped it and screamed. They struggled. She hit him in the leg with a hammer. He tore it out of her hands and threw it down on the garage floor. According to *him*, she tripped over the hammer, hit her head on the tool bench and died immediately. He took a boat from behind the McFarland's house over to Pelican Island and buried her there. He lost the gold bracelet somewhere along the way, left town in Arthur Buckley's van, and dumped it somewhere in Alabama a couple days later."

"And he just told the agent in Georgia all this?" I asked skeptically.

"Yep. How he explained it, he's a drunk and a thief, but he's no murderer. He wanted to set the records straight that it was an *accident*."

I stared out the car window. "Wow. Stacy McFarland was just in the wrong place at the wrong time. To die instantly, she must've damaged her brain stem." Shaking my head, I said, "All these years, Bob's been thinking that Arthur was a murderer. He went to all that trouble to cover for him, getting Chester to commit several crimes along the way, and Arthur didn't even do it."

Agent Watts shook his head. "Criminals are stupid."

I laughed. "I can't wait to see the Buckleys' faces when they hear this."

Agent Watts turned to look at me. "What about Hannah?"

My shoulders slumped. "I don't know. I want to see this to the end. Hannah and I worked really hard."

"That's right. The *two* of you worked *together*." Watts raised his eyebrows, steering me toward the choice I didn't want to make.

I grumbled. "Is this what it's going to be like from now on? Always having to think about someone else?"

Watts nodded. "It's what friends do."

I opened the car door and stumbled into unchartered territory with Watts's words playing in my head.

Before I could ring the doorbell, Hannah opened the door, put her hands on my shoulders and kissed me, right on the lips.

She released her arms as quickly as she'd ambushed me and said, "Took you long enough!"

44

Several court rulings have upheld a person's First Amendment rights to videotape police officers doing their jobs. You have the right to film police in public spaces, including government buildings. Police cannot confiscate or demand to see your video unless they have a warrant. They cannot delete your photos or videos. As videoing has become more common, incidents of police misconduct regularly appear in the news. See Forensics 411 *episode 28, "Smile, You're on Camera."*

IT WAS my first kiss and I wasn't even sure I'd participated. Because I didn't know what to say or do, I blinked twice and told her the news on Monty St. Clair.

Hannah looked at her watch and said, "We've got to go. It's already 12:27."

"But I thought you were too upset. You said you'd had enough."

She put her hands on her hips. "I went soft there for a minute… I had a little breakdown. Guns are scary. But I'm back. I need to see the Buckleys eat crow!"

"Really?" I asked, feeling even more confused. "What about your mom? Did she see you all upset?"

"Nope. She and Josey are out. Let's get out of here before they come back!"

She grabbed my hand and yanked me out her front door.

———

WE ARRIVED at the back of the police station at 12:53 with an arsenal in my backpack: the original McFarland file, the photos on my phone, and Hannah's tablet with Chester Buckley's phone conversations recorded on it.

Hannah and I peeked around from the side of the building. Agent Watts was sitting in his car in the front parking lot right next to Chief Buckley's patrol car. We passed two state troopers in the parking lot across the street, and two more up the block.

At 1:03 a ShipQuick truck pulled up to the main doors of the station. Chief Buckley came out, glanced over his shoulders, and fidgeted while the driver opened the back door of the truck.

Chief Buckley led the delivery man in the front of the building. After they were inside, Agent Watts got out of his vehicle and followed them. We heard him say "hello" to the delivery man as they passed each other in the parking lot.

As soon as Watts was in the building, Hannah and I dashed along the front of the station and sneaked through the front entrance. With Agent Watts's back to us, we tiptoed down a short hallway that ran perpendicular to the front doors. We listened to them from around the corner.

Watts said, "Good afternoon, Chief Buckley."

"Wh-what are you doing here?" he stammered.

"I'm curious about that package you just got."

"It's not mine," the chief said. "It just came. My secretary is always having her personal stuff sent here to the station."

At that moment, a tiny woman with gray hair and watery blue eyes came through the front entrance. She carried a tote bag advertising the *Vista Point Voice*, our local newspaper.

"Who's that?" Hannah whispered.

I shrugged my shoulders. Vista Point was a small town, but not so little that I knew everyone.

The woman approached Watts and Buckley. "Hello," she said. "Chief Buckley, I'm Louise Bacon with the *Vista Point Voice*. I've been trying to get in touch with you all day. You're a hard man to reach."

Hannah and I looked at each other. Louise Bacon was one of the reporters to whom we'd sent the photos of the skeleton. We eased around the corner toward the conversation.

"It's actually not a good time, Ms. Bacon," Watts said, stepping behind the front counter to stand beside the police chief.

"I told you. It's not mine," Chester insisted.

"It has your name on it," Watts said, pointing to the address label.

With our backs against the wall, Hannah and I inched closer to the front counter.

"I'll just have a seat in the lobby until you can speak to me," the reporter said.

She settled in one of several chairs near the entrance and gave us a curious look.

I took out my phone, found her contact information, and texted her a message from across the tiled floor: `Plze don't let on that you see us. We're the ones that sent you the picture of the skeleton.`

Her phone beeped. She took it out of her tote bag, read the text, and gave us a slight nod.

I typed: `You might want to record what is about to happen.`

She read the message, nodded, clicked on a few icons, adjusted the volume on her phone and held it casually above her lap, facing the chief and Agent Watts.

We heard someone open the box. "Why Chief Buckley, it appears that ShipQuick just delivered you a box of bones."

Louise Bacon aimed a questioning look in our direction. Hannah and I nodded.

The reporter stood up and glided toward the front counter. "I happen to be here to question Chief Buckley about some bones." She looked at the police chief. "Is that the same skeleton that Hank Boyd and his dog found over on Pelican Island?"

Chief Buckley turned red and stammered. "I-I-I don't know what you're talking about."

I stepped around the corner, so the chief and Agent Watts could see me, but was careful not to make eye contact with Agent Watts, just in case looks really could kill. Hannah followed.

"No, Ms. Bacon, that is not the same skeleton that my dog found on Pelican Island about two weeks ago."

Agent Watts put his hand up to silence me. Our eyes met, and he shot a piercing glare that communicated his displeasure with our presence at the police station, and the fact that we'd sent pictures of the skeleton to the press.

I thought for sure he was going to kick us out, but instead, he said, "Have a seat, you two."

"Don't mind if we do," Hannah said. She took my hand and pulled me around the front counter and plopped down at the desk behind Agent Watts. I took the one behind Chief Buckley.

Again, Watts's eyes were not happy. If Dr. B were there, he'd hold Watts up as a glowing example of someone who really knew how to use non-verbal communication effectively.

"Just so you know, I'm recording all of this," Louise Bacon said. Agent Watts's shoulders slumped.

He said, "Chief Buckley I am taking you into custody under suspicion of obstruction of justice, conspiracy and evidence tampering." He read him his Miranda rights and put him in handcuffs.

"What? I didn't do anything. I don't even know where that box came from!"

I stood and read the box, "Says here they came from The Bone Room in Los Alamitos, California." I shook my head. "I had no idea such a place existed. That's awesome!"

He sneered at me. "You little…"

"Meddling kids!" Hannah said bouncing in her seat. "*Please* call us meddling kids. Pretty, pretty, please!"

I tried to not laugh at her *Scooby-Doo* reference, but I just couldn't help myself.

A few minutes later, two state troopers escorted Mayor Buckley into the station.

I explained the box of bones to Louise Bacon, speaking loud enough that the Buckleys could hear me.

"Hannah and I believe that Chief Buckley, under the direction of his brother, Mayor Bob Buckley, burned the skeleton that my dog found on Pelican Island. For some reason, they don't want the state crime lab to identify it. The chief and mayor planned to sneak the skeleton in the box to the morgue and say that it was the one that my dog and I found."

"You can't prove that," Chester said.

"Shut up!" the mayor told him. "Don't say anything. You're a cop, you know better!"

"Am I wrong Chief Buckley? Did someone *else* destroy the skeleton I found on Pelican Island?" I asked.

Hannah piped in. "Is it because you thought it was Stacy McFarland?"

Chester's head jolted to the side, and he glared at his older brother.

"Don't… say… anything!" Bob growled at his brother through tight lips.

———————

HANNAH and I waited around for hours while Watts made phone calls and agents questioned the Buckleys. Around six in the evening, Watts made a public statement from inside the police station. Reporters and cameras filled every empty space. Hannah and I stood off to the side while Agent Watts talked.

He stepped forward to introduce himself. "Earlier today, the

SBI charged Vista Point police chief, Chester Buckley, and his brother, the Mayor of Vista Point, Bob Buckley Jr., with obstruction of justice, conspiracy, and tampering with evidence. These charges all stem from the 1985 disappearance of Stacy McFarland. The investigating officer in that case was the current mayor, Bob Buckley Jr."

The reporters whispered to each other.

"Who?"

"Did he say *Tracy* or *Stacy*?"

"I think he said *Kasey*."

Again, the whispers.

"What's he talking about?"

"1985?"

Stacy McFarland was not a case with which the younger news people were familiar.

However, Louise Bacon, the older, seasoned reporter had covered the story decades before. While the other reporters scrambled for information on Stacy, sixty-year-old Louise Bacon, a step ahead of all the others, got the scoop of a lifetime.

Agent Watts explained how Chaucer dug up the bones, how we sent them to the SBI for DNA testing, and got Stacy's hairbrush from her mother for comparison. "Thanks to the keen investigative skills of Hank Boyd and Hannah Simmons, we now know that Stacy McFarland did not run away from home three decades ago. She was killed during a home invasion on the night of June 5, 1985."

Both Buckleys sucked in air, apparently shocked that Agent Watts knew Stacy's fate. After a brief jaw drop, Mayor Buckley stood in stone-faced defiance, and Chester hung his head so low you could see his bald spot.

"Using physical and DNA evidence found near the McFarland's former home, we were able to trace the robbery to an 80-year-old Georgia inmate named Monty St. Clair," Watts announced.

The Buckley's turned to Agent Watts and despite themselves said, "What?"

I leaned over and whispered to them, "That's right. Monty St. Clair robbed the McFarlands and killed Stacy, *by accident.* Arthur had nothing to do with it."

Chester, with his hands cuffed behind his back, tried to shove Bob with his shoulder. "You had me dig up the body, burn the bones, send Corker to Bollywood, and Arthur didn't even do it!"

Bob elbowed Chester in the side. "Shut up, you idiot!"

Bob spoke up to the crowd, seething. "Chester doesn't know what he's talking about. He's mentally unstable, always has been. Mama cut his meat for him 'til he was seventeen! He has absolutely no comment!"

Agent Watts looked like he was about to lose it. Loudly he said, "Um, Chief, Mayor, I wasn't kidding. You really *do* have the right to remain silent."

Chester erupted. The television cameras held steady on him, documenting it all. "You know what? I *would* like to make a comment!" He looked directly at the reporters. "All my life I've taken orders from Bob. *He's* the one that told me to get rid of the skeleton! I didn't know who it was. In fact, Bob didn't even know for sure if it was the McFarland girl. *He* found those two bums and paid them to pretend they were the CSI team. He ordered those new bones on the internet!"

Bob looked stunned, then comical as he tried to kick and punch Chester with his hands cuffed behind his back.

I whispered to Hannah, "Chester just confessed to covering up the existence of the skeleton and implicated Bob in the conspiracy. Prosecution is gonna be a piece of cake. They'll be in the big house just like Helen Tate."

Hannah's head jolted in my direction. "*What* did you say?"

"They'll be in the big house like Helen Tate," I repeated with a triumphant grin.

"What do *you* know about Helen Tate?"

"I'm the *Forensics 411* detective." I arched my eyebrows in a cool, non-verbal-communication-kind-of-way.

Her faced reddened, and her shoulders began to shake.

"You *researched* me?" Her voice got louder. "You freakin' investigated me?"

I looked around. The room went silent, and the reporters stared at us.

She pushed me aside and ran out the door of the police station.

"Hannah! Wait! Come back. I'm sorry!" It was the first time an apology had come so easily. As I chased her out the door, I called, "I didn't know you'd be mad at me. I saw a note in your yearbook from your teacher when I was helping you unpack your boxes. I got curious."

She stopped in the parking lot and turned around with fury in her magical eyes. "Curious? You were *curious*? You read a private letter in my yearbook, and then you did what? Googled me?"

"I found your brother's obituary in the online *Pittsburgh Gazette*. That's in the public domain." I took a deep breath. "It must have been pretty terrible how he died."

"Are there *good* ways for a nine-year-old to die?"

"Um… I guess not…"

"That was a rhetorical question, you—If I'd wanted you to know, I would've told you!"

"But you sort of did. You gave me hints, and Dr. Blanchard says that sometimes a person tells you part of the truth because they want you to know the whole truth, but don't know how to say it."

Crap! I hadn't meant to say that. Only Mom and Grandpa knew I saw Dr. Blanchard.

Her whole body snapped back. "*Dr. Blanchard*? When did you talk to him? He had no right…" Her voiced drifted off.

"But wait!" My lips pursed. "*You* know Dr. Blanchard?"

Her faced reddened, and she glared at me. "None of your

freaking business, you traitor!" She stomped away. After a few yards, she turned around and yelled, "By the way, Boomer is a stupid name. It suits you perfectly!"

I watched her disappear down the road on her bike.

"Crap!" I muttered, collapsing on the curb. I rhythmically punched my leg with my fist. "Stupid, stupid, stupid! You screwed up the only good thing you've ever had in your entire life! You just couldn't help yourself, could you? Chasing people away is your freaking superpower! Why can't you just keep your mouth shut!"

I took a deep breath and counted, *uno, dos, tres...* while I moved the pebbles and gravel around with my feet, trying to make sense of what I'd done. I reached *cincuenta*, and I drew her name in the rock dust then wiped it away.

45

W idely scattered bruises and cuts suggest a struggle or torture took place. See Forensics 411 *episode 24, "Bruises and Contusions."*

THE DOORBELL RANG that night while I was reading the comments on my *Forensics 411* page. I was up to nine hundred ninety-two followers.

I jumped up to answer the door, hoping it was Hannah. I'd texted her every hour since she'd left me at the police station. I'd apologized. I'd explained. I'd begged and groveled. She ignored me.

Officer Corker stood on the front porch, flanked by two state troopers. He had a swollen eye, cut-up face, and bruises everywhere I could see.

"It's Corker," I yelled to Mom and Grandpa.

Mom clambered to the door, a little too quickly if you ask me.

"Oh, my gosh, are you okay?" She took his hand and pulled him through the front door.

"I think so." He looked at the troopers who had escorted him. "It's okay fellas. You can leave me here."

Mom led a limping Steve into our den.

"You look like something from my shower drain," Grandpa said.

Corker took a gulp of water that Mom gave him. "I woke up on a dirt road out in the country. I don't remember anything. They took me to the hospital, and while I was waiting in the ER, the news said that the chief and mayor were arrested."

I told him what I knew of his kidnapping, Rodney Buckley, and the other events of the day, careful not to mention the gun. That would be a secret kept between Hannah, Agent Watts, and me—at least until the Buckley trial.

46

Survivor's Guilt is a mental condition that occurs when a person believes they have done something wrong by surviving a traumatic event when others did not. It is common in combat situations, and we see it more as the number of mass shootings in America increases. See Forensics 411 *episode 41, "Guns and Mass Shootings."*

AFTER BREAKFAST, I went outside and sat on the porch with Chaucer. We opened a package from Mrs. McFarland. Inside was an envelope addressed to my mom, a huge gift basket full of dog toys and treats for Chaucer, and cards for Hannah and me. Mine had a crisp hundred-dollar bill that I would use for my DNA test.

I took Hannah's envelope to her house. Her mom answered the door, looking exhausted. "Hannah's... not feeling well," she said.

I wondered if she was telling the truth or if Hannah just didn't want to see me.

"Can you give her this?" I asked, handing her the envelope. "It's from Mrs. McFarland."

"Of course," she answered with a gentle smile.

"I'm really sorry about your son," I said. "That must've been awful."

"Oh?" She looked surprised. "Hannah told you?"

"Um, yeah." *Sort of.*

"Well, that's good news if she talked to you about it. She must really trust you. She took Ben's death extremely hard. We all did. It was an accident, but Hannah blamed herself."

I had read the account of Ben's death in the Pittsburgh newspaper. When he was in third grade, and Hannah in fifth, he was standing on the sidewalk in front of his school when Helen Tate, an eighty-two-year-old woman, drove up on the curb and hit him and two other kids with her car. Ben died from his injuries. The other two survived. Helen Tate had a blood alcohol level of 1.2, which meant she was incredibly drunk. In court, she said she accidentally hit the gas rather than the brakes, as if she were just some doddering grandma, not a wasted woman with a history of drunk-driving offenses. They sentenced her to five years in prison.

"Hannah usually met Ben at his classroom, and they waited on the sidewalk together for me to pick them up. That afternoon she was late. Ben was standing too close to the road. Hannah thought she could've done something to prevent it if she'd been with him rather than her friends." Mrs. Simmons shook her head slowly. "She was broken for a long time."

I nodded as if I knew the story well.

"We moved here for a fresh start—to get away from the memories. We were so excited when she met you. You took her under your wing and eased the transition to a new place. You're the first friend she's had in years. The kids back home didn't know how to relate to her after Ben's death. She missed a lot of school. When she finally returned, middle school had started, and the kids had moved on without her. She felt even more left out and isolated. The depression got so bad we had to put her in the hospital."

I nodded. Left out, I could understand. Missing months of

school. Broken. Disassembled by circumstances beyond your control. I'd been there in sixth grade.

Hannah and I had the same story.

"It's a major breakthrough that she talked to you about Ben." She patted my shoulder. "She's lucky to have you."

A lump formed in my throat. "Please tell her I'm sorry. She'll know what I mean."

"I will. See you soon, okay?" she said as she closed the door.

I walked down her front steps feeling more confused than ever.

47

The role of a clinical psychologist is to develop a rapport with a patient so the patient opens up, allowing the psychologist to develop a treatment plan based on the patient's needs. They do not morally judge their patient. The goal of the forensic psychologist is the exact opposite. Their job is not to treat the patient but rather to analyze the patient's personality and understand motive for the patient's criminal behavior. See Forensic 411 *episode 18, "Forensics for the Living."*

MOM TOOK the morning off work, and she and Grandpa went with me to the WBCH-TV studio in downtown Wilmington to tape their "Hometown Heroes" segment. Hannah and I were that week's featured heroes. As we crossed the parking lot, Mrs. Simmons's minivan passed us. I smiled, and she looked away in the most obvious way possible.

Mom grabbed my elbow. "Wasn't that Hannah?"

"Yeah."

"We should wait for her."

I shook my head. "Let's just go in. It's hot out here. I don't want to sweat all over my good shirt."

Mom shrugged. "Okay."

An assistant news producer met us right inside the entrance of the building, and led us down a long hallway. "So, Hank, it's always tough for young men, but we need to put a little bit of makeup on you to cut down on the glare from the lights and cameras. It's basically just powder to match the color of your skin."

The makeup lady, named Heather, sat me in a barber chair and tucked a piece of tissue paper in the collar of my shirt. She studied my face for a moment and said, "I think you're probably Walnut 3," and reached for a tub of something and a brush. "Okay, shut your eyes for me, Sugar."

I did as told, and she dusted my forehead with a brush.

When I opened my eyes, Hannah, Mrs. Simmons, and Josey were coming through the doorway. I heard Hannah scoff.

When I looked in her direction, she curled her lip at me and turned away.

"No," Heather said, "Let's try Walnut 2. It's just a smidge lighter. Shut your eyes again."

With my eyes closed, I wished that Hannah would forgive me.

"Perfect," the makeup artist said.

I opened my eyes, and she was messing with my hair.

"Gosh, you've got a great head of hair," she said. "The boys always get the thick waves and long eyelashes."

"I know. It's not fair," my mom agreed. Then noticing Hannah, she said, "Hey, Hannah, long time no see."

"Hi, Ms. Boyd," Hannah said with a tiny smile. She was wearing an outfit I'd never seen before, and her straightened hair looked about six inches longer than usual. "This is my mom, Jennifer Simmons."

My mom and Hannah's shook hands and exchanged pleasantries about how great it was to finally meet each other. Both had enjoyed getting to know the other's child over the summer, blah, blah, blah.

"Have a seat, Hun," Heather said, addressing Hannah. "You're next."

She took the piece of tissue paper out of my shirt collar and announced that I was all done. "Go on out in the hall, and the assistant producer will take you to the studio so you can meet George and Brittany." They were the evening news anchors.

The studio had two sections. One was a big desk where they did the nightly news and then off to the side was a fake living room set, where they usually did interviews.

A couple of minutes later Hannah came in with her mom, Josey and her dad had joined them.

Mr. Simmons waved from across the studio. "Hank, how you doing? Did you ever think you and Hannah would be on television? This is pretty exciting stuff!"

"Hi, Mr. Simmons," I said. "You've met my mom and grandpa, right?"

He shook hands with them. "Sure did, the day you found the body. Nice to see you again…"

Mom pointed at herself. "Angela. And my dad is Henry."

"Right, right," Mr. Simmons said. "How 'bout our little local heroes?"

The longer her dad talked, the farther back Hannah slipped into the corner. Pretty soon she'd be in the hallway.

Then George Chung and Brittany Hernandez came in and introduced themselves to our parents, and then to me. "Now, which one is Hannah?" the female anchor asked.

"I am," Hannah answered from the shadows.

"Well, come on over here. You two will sit next to each other on the couch. I'll be in this chair." She pointed. "George will be in that one. We'll start by introducing you and asking you when, where, and how you found the skeleton. We've enlarged the photos you sent us, and those will show up on that screen right there." She pointed again. "We'll also display the large photo of your dog so that he gets his due credit."

"Now don't be nervous," George Chung said. "This isn't live, so if you mess up, we can just do it again. We've got editors that can splice the whole thing together at the end. It will show on the five o'clock news tomorrow evening."

"Any questions?" Brittany Hernandez asked.

"I have one," Hannah said while stepping out into the studio lights. "Do I have to sit on the couch beside him? Can't one of you sit next to him and I sit in one of the chairs?"

"Hannah!" Mrs. Simmons stepped toward her and yanked her away for a moment.

When they returned, Hannah walked onto the pseudo-living room stage with her arms crossed so tight they might just grow together. She didn't sit. "I'll just wait until you're ready to film," she said.

Grandpa leaned toward me and whispered, "I don't know what happened, but that girl is madder than a snake staring down the business end of a shovel. Whatever it was, you better fix it."

I shook my head. "I don't think I *can* fix it," I whispered back to Grandpa.

During the interview, the news anchors had to keep reminding Hannah to relax, try to look happier, and scoot closer to me on the couch. As soon as the interview was over, she bolted off the sofa and out the studio.

48

When an individual faces information that does not coincide with his worldview, he is likely to find a way to discredit the new information as an attempt to resolve the unease that the information creates in his mind. Likewise, if someone tries to change that person's opinion, the person will often become even more convinced that their view is correct. This is known as the Boomerang Effect. It can affect the investigation process as negatively as confirmation bias. See Forensics 411 episode 40, "Tunnel Vision."

I SAT on the porch with Chaucer and rubbed his ears as he selected a beef-flavored bone from his gift basket of goodies.

"Do you know what today is?" I asked him.

He stopped chewing and inched toward me, putting his head in my lap.

"The last day of summer vacation. We won't get to spend every day together anymore. Worst of all, I don't know what's gonna happen with Hannah." At least I pretended I didn't know.

"She hasn't called or texted since before the police station. She didn't say a word to me during our interviews with the TV news and press." She looked past me like I was invisible, just like the other kids at school. "The popular kids will like her. She'll see how things are for me at school, and I'll be eating lunch alone in the media center as usual."

He thumped his tail on the deck. "No, that's not good. It means that I'm alone, just like always. Everyone will want to be her friend, and she's not stupid, she'll do the math. I've basically shoved her into the popular crowd."

"I think you're mistaken about that, Hank," Mom said as she came out the screened door, finally getting my new name right.

She sat next to me on the deck. "I was eavesdropping on you and Chaucer, and I think that you have it all wrong. I've seen you two this summer. Hannah is a true friend." She bumped my shoulder with hers. "She's a keeper."

"But it'll change once school starts. She'll figure out that no one likes me."

"*She* likes you. And this year might be different. It's high school. There'll be lots of new people. Kids mature over the summer. You're not the same person you were in June. In fact, you're practically a celebrity after all your detective work this summer." Mom smiled. "Be optimistic."

"I messed up. Hannah and I had a huge fight. It's over, and there's no way to make it un-over."

"True friends can fight, forgive, and still be friends. You know, like your boomerang. She'll come back. Just give her time."

I shook my head. "This was really bad."

"Apologize. Own your mistake. Tell her you're sorry. It's a show of strength, not weakness. You might be pleasantly surprised."

Mom kissed me on the cheek and stood up. "Now, do you want me to cut that hair for the first day of school? It's so long." She smiled. "I'd forgotten how thick and wavy your hair is. It's like..."

"Like what?" I asked.

She rearranged herself on the deck. "It's handsome," she answered.

The dialogue door was there, right between us. All I had to do was open it. Just a crack.

Turn the knob, peek inside and ask about my father.

Do I have hair like my father? That's all I needed to say.

"Um... I."

The daddy dialogue door slammed shut.

"I spent the summer growing out my buzz-cut, and I think I'm going to leave it longer. Can you take me to a professional and get it cut into an actual style? If I'm going to start high school with a new name, I might as well have a new look, too."

Mom smiled. "Sure, Sweetie. Let's leave in about a half hour."

I stood up. "I'll be in my room."

49

Stacy McFarland was a sixteen-year-old girl who disappeared from her home in Vista Point, North Carolina on June 5, 1985. The investigating officer, Bob Buckley Jr., purposely botched the investigation and fabricated evidence to make it look like Stacy ran away from home so he could draw suspicion away from his own brother. For the whole story, see Forensics 411 *episode 45, "Vanished in Vista Point."*

I LOOKED straight into the video camera and spoke. "*Forensics 411:* Episode 45, Vanished in Vista Point." My monologue wouldn't make it to the final cut, but I had some things I needed to say. Dr. B called it "closure," even though the last thing I wanted with Hannah was a conclusion.

"I'm sorry… for everything." I glanced at my dark paneled walls. "If no one's told you yet, I'm not a local celebrity. I'm about as far from that as you can get." I sighed. "To me, you were more than just a person I met or the friend I'd been waiting for my entire life, you were an event. You divided my life into before and after."

I felt a small lump form in my throat, so I waited until it went away. "Obviously, I *never* meant for you to get hurt on the island.

I should've told you just to stay put." I shook my head with regret. "But it was really nice of you to go looking for Chaucer. It was something a friend would do."

I read the *X-Files* poster that hung on the wall opposite my bed: The Truth is Out There. Time for the big one, the grand-daddy of all mistakes. "About Helen Tate. I'm sorry. You're right, I shouldn't have investigated you. That was wrong. I haven't told anyone about Ben, or any of it, and I swear, I never will."

Who would I tell? She was my only friend. "And you shouldn't feel guilty about Ben. It was an accident. You're strong. In fact, I think you must be the strongest person I know."

I let out a deep breath. "I wanted to solve the McFarland case." Staring back into the camera I said, "No, scratch that—*we* wanted to solve the case... together—the two of us." I looked down. Life was a lot easier before I knew what it was like to lose a friend.

"Hank," Mom yelled from the kitchen, "Come on, let's go get that haircut!"

I stopped the video recorder, took a deep breath, and called over my shoulder, "Be there in a second."

50

S *cientific evidence shows that forgiveness actually improves physical and mental health. Failing to forgive a person of wrong-doing can cause the non-forgiver to experience elevated cortisol levels, increased adrenaline and chronic pain. See* Forensics 411 *episode 32, "Understanding the Victim."*

I STOOD at the intersection between my house and Hannah's, overwhelmed with dread. I whispered to myself, "It's a new year, a new school, a new bus. Maybe Dillon moved to Yemen. Your new haircut looks awesome, the lady at Snippy Scissors said so. You've got a thousand followers on Twitter and two thousand subscribers to *Forensics 411*. You're the tenth most popular forensic blogger on the web. You're practically trending."

Then I heard the bus.

I hated the bus.

The yellow doors opened. My same bus driver was back with her coffee breath and thinning hair. She seemed as unhappy to be there as I was.

I got on and quickly pushed through the aisle to an empty seat about half-way back.

I sat down fast and looked out the window. The driver pulled away from my stop then slammed on the brakes. She opened the doors and Hannah climbed aboard.

She looked different. Was she wearing makeup? Her hair, tamed into smooth golden waves, fell over her shoulders. Large block letters across her chest identified the maker of her shirt.

She looked like one of *them*. The metamorphosis had begun.

As Hannah surveyed the crowd, I lowered my eyes to spare us both.

I glanced up for a second as she pushed through the narrow aisle, bumping kids' arms and backpacks as she made her way toward the back of the bus. She raised her hand above shoulder-height and moved it right, then left, then right again.

A wave.

"Can I sit here?" she asked, standing beside me.

"Um, sure," I answered pulling my backpack off the seat.

After she sat, she said, "You know, in most western societies, when someone waves at you, you're supposed to wave back. Do we need to review that *again*?"

"Nope," I answered, smiling back. "I'm good."

She nodded. "Me, too."

ABOUT THE AUTHOR

Whitney Verdin Skeen grew up in rural Lancaster County, Pennsylvania before cable television. With only three fuzzy channels to watch, and no air conditioning, she found solace in books. She spent her favorite summer days at the air-conditioned public library where she browsed the shelves for the perfect story, and found it many times over. Those library days inspired her first literary work, *The Mouse That Couldn't Eat Cheese*, back in second grade. She went on to graduate from the University of North Carolina at Chapel Hill and become a middle school teacher. For years, she witnessed the intense and erratic world that middle schoolers navigate daily. Those observations inspired her to create Hank, Hannah and the cast of characters that inhabit Vista Point. Today Whitney lives on the coast of North Carolina with her husband, two sons, and the dogs that love them. *Vanished in Vista Point* is her first novel.

www.WhitneySkeen.com

Follow Whitney on Facebook.com/AuthorWhitneySkeen
and Twitter @WhitneySkeen

If you enjoyed this book and would like to read more adventures by Hank, Hannah, and Chaucer, please have an adult help you do one or more of the following:

- Leave a review on your favorite book review site
- Tell a friend about the book and author
- Ask your local library to put Whitney Skeen's work on the shelf
- Recommend Fawkes Press books to your local bookstore
- Sign up for our First Looks & Freebies newsletter

Readers make our books possible!

FAWKES PRESS

CPSIA information can be obtained
at www.ICGtesting.com
Printed in the USA
BVHW030046131220
595588BV00028B/451